THE DAY BEFORE YOU CAME

Matthew Cash

BURDIZZO BOOKS

Published in Great Britain in 2022 by Matthew Cash Burdizzo Books Walsall, UK

The Day Before You Came

Foreword

Ghosts.

They're strange things, aren't they?

Fascinating things.

I learned whilst reading (better name my source as it's a great read and it will make me sound totes intelli', bro) A Natural History of Ghosts: 500 Years of Hunting For Proof by Roger Clarke, that one of our stereotypical, and now somewhat cartoonish, images of a ghost—I'm talkin' about the sheets— comes from corpses being wrapped in burial shrouds, pre-1750. That book is a must for anyone who's interested in spooks and what they might or might not be.

I personally don't believe in them. But I want to. I don't understand why anyone would hate the idea of ghosts, surely the idea that there's more than just this life is something to cling to? But still I don't believe in them.

I've had experiences, as detailed in The Cash Compendium & Continuity, that I still can't satisfactorily explain, but which I put down to my own crazy head— and yet I'm still a sceptic.

I've lost both parents, two sisters, uncles, aunties, and cousins to Death's unbiased hand and not had any return visits, although most of these people were just as anti-social whilst alive, so...

Obviously that doesn't disprove ghosts' existence; they might just be having a whale of a time and not give two shits about what we're doing down here.

Despite my scepticism, I've always been fascinated by the supernatural and I think the ultimate jewels are the things we cannot debunk, those are the little twinkles that make you feel like a scared, excited kid again, and there are quite a few strange, inexplicable occurrences that fit into that category.

Why is it you can randomly think about someone you've not thought of for months, years even, and then BAM, walking around the corner, here they come?

How is it that some buildings hold some sort of atmosphere? You can automatically feel safe somewhere and it's not always to do with home security and location. Or vice versa.

Why is it you can go somewhere you've never been before and somehow you know where stuff is, or you get strong feelings of déjà-vu?

The majority of ghosts that have haunted me, or continue to do so, are the memories of people who are still very much alive and kicking, but who are not in my life anymore.

They've left my existence and are in some After-MattyBob-Life that I know nothing about unless I catch random glimpses of them between crowds of Saturday shoppers.

I'm Haunted by times I miss, regret, or which I just want to reminisce about.

Haunted by a bus diversion that inadvertently goes down the road where *they* lived and stirs up memories I thought long buried.

Haunted by the sting in the corner of my eyes whenever I think about the good experiences I had with someone.

Haunted by the things you might have been able to do and say to have kept them in your life.

Haunted by the things I wished I could have said, but which I was too scared to say at the time.

I'm haunted by the ghosts of my past a lot; they love showing up on Christmas day.

I have more spectral visitors than Ebenezer.

This book stemmed from an idea I had about six years ago. I'm a big Irvine Welsh fan and one day I asked myself, 'What would Begbie do in the Amityville Horror?' He is an insanely fearless character who seems to laugh in the face of most adversity and would never back down from a fight no matter what the odds were.

When I worked at Butlins in 2001, I knew this bloke who thought he was a big hard man, had the whole Begbie attitude (aside from the fact that he rarely started the fights, and was, overall a lovely guy), and I would always secretly take the piss by asking him completely irrational questions regarding his bravado.

What would you do if a ninja came after you?

What would you do if three ninjas came after you, one had a sword, one had a gun, and the other had a feather duster?

What would you do if twenty ninjas, naked, came after you? (Not all of my hypothetical questions contained ninjas but you get the gist.) And his reply would always be 'I'd go fucking schiz' on 'em, mate!' and he'd throw some moves he remembered from watching the Karate Kid trilogy.

If you know who Begbie is, portrayed by Robert Carlyle in the Trainspotting films, what do you think he would do against an invisible force? Against a haunted house? Against something he couldn't understand, or even see, and more importantly for someone like him, something he couldn't physically hurt?

As ever, with my initial thoughts and what they turn into, this book morphed into something I wasn't really expecting. That's kind of how I write, how I live. I have the basics in my head and make it up as I go along, trying the best I can. It's exciting, and a little unnerving, not quite knowing what's around the corner, but luckily, in fiction, I can rewind, erase, and do it again if it doesn't work out.

Lastly, I'd like to add that I would love to experience more supernatural stuff: I love it, it scares me, even though I don't believe it's genuinely what my brain tells me it is, so to any ghosts reading this, feel free to drop by, preferably in the daytime and not the cold, dark of night, and say 'Howdy, motherfucker.'

Ghosts and the supernatural will always be cool to this horror fan.

Matty-Bob
August 1st 2022

Dedication

To everyone still haunted by the past.

Disillusion

Houses don't need to be frequented by spectres to qualify as haunted. They can be plagued by invisible memories, emotions, repercussions of Life's eternal drumbeat. Like sunlight and rain, hatred can weather the walls; poison can raise roof tiles. Words creeping and clinging, ivy on the brickwork, invasive. Thoughts and feelings can soak into the wallpaper like nicotine, leaving stains that last for decades, remnants for future occupants.

Ghosts don't have to be dead people, merely echoes of those who are gone or lost — but who are not entirely forgotten.

Part 1: Bumblebee

One of Us

"I can't hear a fucking thing. It's in your bloody head. You're going daft like her out back."

Vera's so used to Roger's abuse that it rarely angers her anymore. She never hears the noise when he's nearby anyway, his heavy breathing puts paid to that.

"Want to see what I got from doing my rounds?" she says, wheeling her shopping trolley past his armchair and unzipping a tartan flap.

"Not particularly," Roger grumbles, and squints through grimy bifocals at a folded newspaper. "More kindling, no doubt."

Vera ignores his putdowns. *Why shouldn't I spend money on things I like?* At least she has something to show for her spending. Roger fritters their money away on fags, beer, and horses. She pulls out a porcelain figure of two children sitting on a bench. "Look at this. Isn't it lovely?" Roger gives it a glance, his rheumy eyes barely visible beneath overgrown eyebrows, and mumbles, "More bloody kids."

Well you never gave me any, did you? Vera thinks, and carefully peels the price sticker from the base of the ornament.

"Still, it'll all go up when the house catches," Roger says, determined to rile her.

"The house is *not* going to burn down." She hates herself for retaliating but sometimes it is the only way to shut him up. Shut him up or at least get him to bugger off to the shed so she can watch her programmes in peace without his brooding and making bitter remarks.

"The house is *not* going to burn down," she repeats, as Roger laughs theatrically, looking up towards the ceiling. The spark is ignited in his eyes, his fuse lit. "The house is not going to burn down? Are you sure about that? With that daft old bugger out back? She almost set fire to the fucking kitchen three years ago when she decided to make toast at three o'clock in the morning. Senile old trout."

Vera takes a deep breath. *He will never let that go.* She hates herself for rising to his bait and decides not to press it. She finds a few spare inches on the sideboard for her new addition.

"Clutter, that's what caused it. Too much shite everywhere." It seems Roger is determined to have his argument regardless of her involvement. "All throughout our marriage all you've ever done is horde shite, Vera, and one day we'll fucking well burn in it."

"I think I'm going to make a soup for tea. Do you fancy chicken, mushroom, or tomato?"

Roger stands up abruptly, newspaper tucked under his armpit. "No, I don't want any fucking soup. I don't want to sit here and watch your mother dribble down her sagging tits whilst you drivel on at her as if she can understand a single word you can say."

"The doctors say it's good —"

"The doctors are all foreigners who don't know their arses from their elbows!"

"We'll have chicken."

"I'm going to the pub. I can't stay in this house any longer."

Vera sighs with relief as the front door slams. She looks at the clock: almost five. *Perfect. Roger won't be back until closing.* A whole evening of peace to look forward to. A few hours to herself once she has got her mum settled for the night. There might be some truth in what Roger says about her mum's capacity for understanding—she hasn't shown any signs of acknowledgement for over a year—but she is still her mum. Besides, even having a one-way conversation with someone who sits staring into space is far more appealing than the prospect of an evening with her husband.

Kindling. Vera grimaces; the word grates. That's what Roger calls the treasures she brings home. She snorts and scowls at a framed black-and-white photo on a sideboard laden with ornaments. With the sun in his eyes, a twenty-two-year-old Roger squints back, jet-black hair, fag-end glued to his lower lip, smile more of a grimace than a grin.

He was handsome back then, but those dark and devilish looks soon faded and now only the devil remains. He hadn't swept her off her feet like all the good men are supposed to do; they'd just met and that was it. Roger had brought their coal; she'd fancied him from the off but it didn't dawn on her how much of a bastard he was until she was forced to marry him.

Her father was the warden of St Francis church, and when Vera suspected she was pregnant, he rushed through their marriage arrangements, even bribing Roger with the money for the deposit on their house. He had been a no-hoper, even back then, but could turn on the charm when he needed to and wasn't going to miss the opportunity to get away from his parents.

She's never truly forgiven her dad for ruining her life. There was no baby then, and there never will be. There is nothing wrong with her, the tests confirmed it. Roger wouldn't get tested, though; it questioned his masculinity. She's only ever broached the subject once, five years after they were wed, when her father died without having been made a grandfather. Roger had given her a black eye and told her to fuck off.

Vera sighs and pulls her shopping trolley through the living room into the kitchen to unload the few tins she has bought. She leaves two chicken soups on the counter before packing everything else away. She takes a loaf from the bread bin and pauses when she hears a low hum.

It's just loud enough for her to question whether she can hear it or whether Roger is right about it being in her imagination. She tries to follow the noise to its source but it's so very faint anything can distract her from it. Her eyes are drawn to the picture rail near the lounge ceiling, and then to the small square loft hatch. If there is something in the attic, she will get Roger to find it next time he insists she has a clear-out. He is as bad as her for hoarding, except everything goes up in the attic in case he might need it someday.

There is no end of junk in the attic, it's his domain, not hers. She isn't allowed up there, Roger says, *not with her fat arse and elephant legs*. He knows where to step, *she'll come through the fucking ceiling like a sack of spuds*.

*

"She'll be festering in front of the box watching Corrie with her mum and fucking knitting," Roger says, draining his ale and placing the dimpled pint glass on the bar next to some loose change.

A thin, practically skeletal man sits beside him, his face so gaunt you can see the contours of every bone and muscle. "I don't know how you put up with it, Rog."

"Why do you think I'm hardly ever home?" He pushes the coins towards a barmaid, who retrieves his glass. He winks at the woman, young and blonde, with a perm. "As soon as her mum kicks the bucket I'll divorce her and move young Tina in. Won't I, sweetheart?"

The barmaid laughs politely, the smile never reaching her eyes, and replaces Roger's drink as he goes over to the cigarette machine.

He sits back down and waits for Tina to move before speaking to his friend. "The dotty old bat is worth a fucking fortune, and all this time the money is being frittered away on looking after her when she's nothing but a fucking vegetable."

"I don't know, Roger." The thin man rubs a hand over his face and stares into his drink. "People will notice if I suddenly come into money. They'll think I've been on the rob again. 'Farrington's up to his old tricks.' I can't deal with going back inside, mate, I'm fucking fifty next year. It nearly killed me last time. I'm not cut out for the nick."

"So, you don't go prancing around flaunting it, do you? Or if you do, you make up some crap about coming up on the pools." Roger offers Farrington the opened cigarette packet.

"And they won't blame you?"

"No. I've got a night away planned with three others.
Shooting, up at Colbear's. I usually do it this time of year
and bring back some pheasant for the freezer to keep Vera
sweet. I'll be there all night. Alibis and what have you."
Farrington rolls the liquid around his glass and holds his
cigarette out for Roger to light it. "Five grand?"
Roger nods. "As soon as that old bat's money goes into
our bank account. I'll have to figure out an excuse for it,
though, although I don't know what."
"Be the doting husband and handle the funeral and all the
expenses?" Farrington says timidly, as though he is afraid
to even suggest it.
Roger leers at his friend. "See? I fucking knew you were a
criminal mastermind."

I'm a Marionette

"Here." Roger hands Farrington a four-pack of beer and a brown paper bag that's speckled with grease spots. Inside the bag are two sausage rolls.

"What's this, you made me a packed lunch? Didn't know you cared, Rog."

"Shut up." Roger grins and takes a stepladder that has been leaning against the living room wall. "You're going to be up there bloody hours, mate."

Farrington sighs and looks up at the ceiling hatch. "Yeah, I hope I don't fall asleep."

"You'll be fucking lucky to find fucking space up there to park your arse comfortably enough."

"Hmm. So, what time is Vera back?" Farrington says, watching Roger climb the ladder.

"She'll be back about half four, always gets the quarter-to bus from town. Regular as clockwork, our Vera. That's one thing you can rely on." Roger slides back two tiny hooks-and-eyes either side of the hatch and pushes a square of wood upwards, revealing the entrance to the attic.

Farrington takes a small rubber torch from his pocket and turns it on and off.

"You know where to step, don't you?" Roger shouts down.

"Yeah, you've told me umpteen times. Stick to the beams." Roger pulls himself up into the darkness. "Pass us that box up, will you?"

A small cardboard box of ornaments wrapped in newspaper sits at the foot of the ladder. Farrington lifts it under one arm and climbs the ladder.

"If she had her way, she'd give all this shite back to the bloody charity shops. Daft cow." Roger takes the box from Farrington and puts it to one side in the darkness of the attic. "At least this way I can flog it next time there's a boot sale."

"You got the right idea, Roger."

"Too bloody right I have," Roger says, leaning back out of the hatch. "Now, get back down there, make sure you don't need a slash or owt, then you can get your arse up here ready."

Whilst Farrington walks through the kitchen towards the toilet, he pictures the events and how they should unfold. Hours of sitting in the cramped, dusty darkness will be the worst part, but at least he has something to eat and drink. He'll wait until ten o'clock, almost six bloody hours in the fucking attic, and when everything is quiet, he'll lift the hatch using the rope handle on its back, and lower himself onto the armchair below.

Farrington is tall, so he will only have about a foot to drop. Then he will go through to the front bedroom and use a cushion or something to smother the mother-in-law, before letting himself out of the front door.

The only sign that anything will be amiss will be that the two hooks-and-eyes on the ceiling side of the hatch would be swinging open, but Roger says he often leaves them undone.

It's a piece of cake.

"Jesus Christ," Roger says, stepping off the ladder, as Farrington comes towards him still fastening the drawstring of his tracksuit trousers. "It's Albert Steptoe, the next generation."

Farrington grins, revealing a mouthful of teeth that are as bad as the fictional rag-and-bone man's, and mimes smoking. "We got time for a quick one before you lock me up for the night?"

"Fuck's sake." Roger begrudgingly takes a tobacco tin out of his shirt pocket and produces a pair of pre-rolled cigarettes. "You're such a scrounging bastard, do you know that?"

Farrington nods proudly and points his cigarette at the hole in the ceiling. "So, have you got any valuables up there?"

"Don't even bloody well think about it, Farrington!" Roger grabs a wedge of the wiry man's jumper.

"I'm pulling your leg, I'm pulling your leg, calm down," Farrington says, puffing cigarette smoke and halitosis into his friend's face.

Roger grimaces; it is the closest he ever gets to a smile. "Fuck-all up there of any worth, just junk. You'd have to clear the lot to make twenty quid, if that. Sometimes I think the place would be better if it did burn down, with us all in it."

"Don't say that, you've got it good, man," Farrington says, his cigarette almost gone already.

"How have I got it good?"

"Wife and a house, for one thing."

Roger rolls his eyes. "A fat old sow and her withered old cabbage of a mother. And a house we can't afford to repair until the cabbage croaks. That's what I've got."

"And your fancy piece you were telling me about, up in Blackton."

Roger is taken aback. "I don't remember telling you about that."

Farrington nods slightly. "Christmas time, remember you came round my flat? We had that whisky I thieved from Chappell's."

"Shit," Roger mutters behind his hand.

"Maybe, we could make it seven grand?" Farrington suggests coldly, but Roger's laughter is icier.

"You honestly think I give a fuck about you telling Vera about Angie?"

Farrington focuses on Roger's belly wobbling as he chuckles. "Let me tell you this, within a year of the wedding, Vera found a pack of French letters in my hunting coat pocket. Sometimes, we have entertainment at Colbear's parties. And you know what? You know what?" Roger pauses and stares at his ratty accomplice.

"What?" Farrington says, avoiding eye contact like a punished child.

"She never said a fucking word." Roger beams triumphantly. "My Vera knows her place, I put her firmly in it when I married her. Now, you get your stinking, bony arse up in that loft right now and get this done and be grateful I don't lower it to two grand."

Farrington skulks past Roger, picks up the sausage rolls and beer, and steps on the bottom rung of the ladder. He turns as he is about to climb, holding the bag of food between his teeth. "Sorry, Rog."

"No you fucking ain't," Roger snaps back.

Farrington climbs up the ladder and into the attic.

Roger watches Farrington close the hatch. "Don't you dare fuck this up!"

Sitting in the Palmtree

Keeping to the beams, Farrington shines the torch around the attic looking for somewhere to sit amongst the boxes and dilapidated furniture. It's cluttered with useless junk. A standard lamp with no shade and a broken bulb lies haphazardly across an avalanche of old blankets and what looks like magazines or newspapers. He can see why Roger kept it: it has a nice decorative stem, solid, well-made, maybe someone will pay a few quid for it if they are in the mind to fix it up, but the majority of the stuff he can see won't fetch much, and if anyone knows anything about flogging shit, Farrington does.

He moves a box labelled 'Mum's Stuff', sits on a beam, and leans against a mountain of blankets and newspapers. The end of the lamp juts out over his head; he loops the wrist strap of his torch around it and chuckles at his makeshift lantern. He's brought a book with him, and spare batteries, needs something to do to while away the hours.
Farrington makes himself comfortable, cracks open a can of beer, and starts reading.

The Day Before You Came

Does Your Mother Know?

There is always a small element of fear whenever Vera approaches the front bedroom. A flash-forward of what might lie behind that door sears across her vision like a blast of sunlight. Her ancient, wrinkled mother, lifeless and cold, beneath layers of blankets.
But Vera is no seer, just an ordinary paranoid daughter with an enduring love for her mother that hasn't dissipated over the fifty-five years of her life. A love that only ever expands, even as she watches the woman shrink, both physically and mentally. This is the woman who'd taught her to knit, who'd taught her to sew half a dozen types of stitches, and the day will come where her vision, or some version of it, will play out.
Vera lives in fear of her own death before her mother's. She is the child now, her dependent, and sometimes she worries herself sick over the idea of her mother being left on her own with Roger. Vera won't put her in a home, not whilst she is able-bodied enough to look after her herself. It isn't right, but she knows he would do so in a heartbeat.

Vera opens the bedroom door, relief sweeping away the dark thoughts as she sees her mother's flabby arm move across the sheets. "Come on, Mother. Tea time. Let's go and have some soup and watch a bit of telly, eh? It's Coronation Street tonight, you know you love your Corrie."

Vera draws the curtains back, ending her mother's afternoon nap, and gently rolls back the blankets. She pats the sheets around her mum's legs, relieved that she is still dry, and rolls a wheelchair beside the bed. "Let's get you to the loo before you go off." Vera carefully sits her up and encourages the sluggish woman to move from the bed to the chair.

She is still heavy despite the weight she has lost over the last few years.

That's one thing she has inherited.

Why couldn't I have been tall and willowy like my father? Vera has never been attractive like her mother, even when she was younger, and she has never had a man as doting as her father.

Vera spends twenty minutes spooning lukewarm soup and chunks of soggy bread into her mother's mouth, before cleaning her up and making her comfortable in front of the television. A pot of tea is set down between them in time for the second greatest soap opera. Vera takes pleasure in seeing her mum turn towards the TV as the theme tune starts. A tiny tremble turns up her thin lips; seconds later, her chin dips and she is asleep.

Vera watches Emmerdale Farm beside her sleeping mother. This is her life now. These are her friends and family. Fictional or not, she laughs when they do and cries when they die. She feels their agonies, shares their glories. It's pathetic, but what else does she have?

*

The table is laid out as if it's Christmas time. A goose, a fucking goose. "Fucking hell, Kevin, you have gone to some trouble tonight, haven't you?" Roger says, straightening his tie as he enters the banqueting hall. He nods to the three other men sitting around the table. Kevin Colbear claps a hand on Roger's rounded shoulder. "Only the best for my friends, Roger, you know that." Colbear is a tall, broad man, well-defined, looks and acts like he is royalty.

"Well, I say 'you', but I doubt this is your handiwork," Roger says with a wink.

"No, you're right, Jan and Grace did all this for us before they took the mother-in-law to some show at the West End, but I did kill the goose." Colbear shows Roger to a seat and pours him a glass of wine. "We'll fill our bellies and crack out the brandy and cigars after the shoot." Roger sips at his drink; he doesn't give a shit about wine but booze is booze. The alcohol content is low, Colbear doesn't want them shooting one another out there on the fields. Roger casts an eye over the bounties on the table, waits for Colbear to sit, before sheepishly asking from behind his wine glass, "Will there be any other entertainment tonight, Kevin?"

Colbear stands over them at the head of the table, fork and carving knife in hand. "That all depends on how good you are at shooting."

*

The smell hits her as soon as she opens the door. A warm, cloying stench that instantly makes her gag. "Oh, Mum."

Her mother sits on the chair, filthy hands dangling limply above her face. Her blankets are askew, her midsection and the surrounding furniture a mess of dark brown. *She only went to make a Pot Noodle.*

"Don't move," Vera says, a bit more sharply than she intends to, but she can't help it. She goes to fetch the plastic laundry hamper and rolls her mother's wheelchair over. Rolling up her sleeves, she pulls her marigolds out of her apron. "Come on, Mother, let's get you cleaned up."

*

Farrington screws up the brown paper bag the sausage rolls came in and shoves it in his trouser pocket. One thing for certain is he can hear every little noise that comes from below. He's heard Vera come and Roger go, heard her demeanour immediately change as soon as her husband left the house. When they were together, all he could hear was quiet mumbling from her, and whining or barking insults, orders from Roger. The words weren't entirely clear but the odd thing slipped up through the floorboards, mostly from Roger's tongue. *Filthy shitting sow!* was one thing Farrington heard as clear as day.

He finishes the last of the beer and quietly stands to stretch out. The boards creak beneath him and he freezes, listening. There is no change to the noises below, still the steady, high volume of the television. Vera can't have heard, or surely, she would have muted the box.

In a way, Farrington pities her, he loathed his mother. She'd had him sent away when she'd caught him standing behind her at the age of eight, her sewing scissors in his hands, ready to bring down into her back. He doesn't know why he did it, only that he had always hated her.

But things were different for Vera, she idolised her mum. He had been there, at Roger and Vera's wedding. Most of Roger's workmates had gone to the reception for the piss-up and buffet; he had been one of the few who had attended the church service. He'd been a lad then, only a couple of years out of the home and in a place of his own, working at the factory with Roger. That was before he had been caught nicking.

It had been a beautiful summer day. The wedding was a traditional white dress affair with all the trimmings, but Vera took ages to get to the church. He'd gone outside for a fag, fed up with sitting inside on such a hot day, and he was there when the bride's car pulled up. The two bridesmaids got out of the vehicle first; one of them had been in tears, and they weren't happy tears. He'd instinctively hidden around the corner of the building to slip back in once the music started playing. That's when he saw Vera in a right old state with her mum, both red-faced and distraught. Vera's dad, a beast of a man, had driven them there. People reckoned he was a fucking psycho even though he was a churchgoer.

Farrington saw mother and daughter in one another's arms, crying, her mother repeatedly telling her father to 'Listen to her,' and Vera saying 'I'm not pregnant' over and over again. Her dad got out and slammed the door so hard Farrington was surprised the windows didn't shatter.

Next, her father stormed around the front of the car as though he was going to kill the pair of them. He never said a word, just thrust his hand towards the church doors and pointed, before brushing down his suit jacket and entering without looking back, having absolute faith that they would obey.

Farrington felt the urge to go to the two women but there was nothing he could do or say, he was already partially shunned in the area for being the man who had tried to kill his mother. He watched as they promptly tidied themselves up, took deep breaths, practised smiling, and entered the building.

Vera's father had died within a year of their wedding and no baby ever showed up.

Now the poor old bastard is stuck with a man she didn't want to marry, looking after the woman who didn't stop her husband from forcing her into it. Farrington wonders how you can live with something like that your whole life. He hopes that after tonight the pair of them will find some kind of middle ground before they die, even though Roger is possibly an even worse specimen of a man than her father ever was.

His muscles are well and truly stretched. He sits back down against the stack of blankets and newspapers and curses when the pile of junk comes down on him. "Fucking hell," Farrington whispers, moving blankets clogged with dust from his face and pushing the broken lamp away. He hears Vera's voice rise below him; she mutes the television.

My Mama Said

"What the bloody hell was that?" Vera places her Pot Noodle on the coffee table. She reaches for the remote and mutes the news; it's boring anyway, she only likes the regional. It sounds like something in the attic. Whatever it was has stopped as abruptly as it began.

She frowns, looking up at the ceiling and the attic hatch. It sounded soft. She tries to remember what is up there that is soft but it is useless, she hasn't been up there for at least fifteen years. She turns back towards the telly and notices that the box of charity items that had been stowed behind the sofa has vanished. "Oh, that explains it," she says to her mother, who is, surprisingly, awake. "Roger's been up there. I bet he's disturbed something."

"Bloody Roger," Vera's mum says, and rolls her eyes, and Vera forgets all about the noise in the attic. That is the horrible thing about her mother's condition, the rare moments where she randomly acts how she used to, but only for a few seconds, a few words, half a phrase or a facial expression. She is like a constantly tuned-out radio which, somehow miraculously, due to some diverse weather condition, picks up on a frequency thought nigh-on impossible, and there comes a brief blip of coherency. Sometimes it makes Vera laugh, but mostly it makes her cry.

She wipes away the tears. The news is over, and Coronation Street is on after the adverts. She reaches over the coffee table, pats her mum's knee, and tells her, "I love you no matter what." As she reaches for the remote, she hears the humming.

Super Trouper

"How many's that you got now, Roger?" Peter Green says, walking beside him across the field. He is a little man, bald and imp-like.

"At least a dozen, I reckon," Roger says, picking up the dead pheasant and putting it in a sack.

"We'll fill his larder up till springtime."

"Reckon we will."

The pair walk through the dark fields. The others are spread out in pairs over the land; the game is abundant, anything that flies into the dusk sky finds gunpowder in it.

"So, you know what Kevin's got up his sleeve for later, Pete?"

A low cackle comes from Roger's fellow shooter. "Yeah, I do."

"Well, come on then, spill the beans."

Peter shakes his head. "Not for me to say, Roger, but I'll tell you this. You know I've got friends in high places?"

"Just because you're mates with some crappy comedian doesn't mean you've got friends in high places," Roger says. Green had once introduced them to his celebrity friend, Suffolk comedian Diddy Dave Diamond, but Roger thought he was a fucking prick. Just because you were a fucking comedian didn't mean you had to crack jokes all the time and laugh at the end of every fucking sentence. He nearly smacked him by the end of the night, the smarmy little prick.

"That might well be, Roger, but if it weren't for Mr. Diamond, Kevin wouldn't have got the connection with the escort agency now, would he? You wouldn't be slapping the arses of beautiful women four or five times a year and feeding your fat belly on good food just for filling Colbear's freezer."

"I suppose he was alright on Crackerjack," Roger mutters. Green nods. "Well, let's just say whilst Colbear's wife, daughter and mother-in-law were in one car going to the city for the night, they would be passing another car coming from the city with several of the agency's finest, youngest ladies."

Roger smiles into the rapidly retreating sunset and thinks about how wonderfully his day is going to end.

Two For the Price of One

What the fuck is that? He hasn't moved at all since the blankets fell on him, other than to push them carefully aside.

A frantic humming comes from nearby. When the pile of junk slides, the lamp upends and the torch lands in his lap beneath the falling layers. He uncovers himself as quietly as possible, finds the torch, and sees the insects zipping past its beam. "Shit," Farrington hisses between gritted teeth. He jumps to his feet and shrieks as the broken lightbulb still in the lamp socket rips at his face.

*

Vera feels her bladder weaken when she hears a muffled scream come from the attic. Even her mother registers the disturbance, turning her face up to the ceiling.

Loud creaking and cracks came from above. Vera stands in the centre of the living room, not knowing what to do when her mother says something about thunder, and the ceiling gives way.

Vera falls to the carpet as Artex, plaster, floorboards, boxes of ornaments, years of unwanted belongings come crashing down on her mother. Something brown, the size and shape of a large watermelon, rolls across the carpet, spilling insects like smoke.

Amidst the debris on top of her mother is a scrawny, middle-aged man. He lands upside down, his head hitting the floor between her mum's feet, his neck twisted at an unnatural angle. Swarms and swarms of wasps pour into the room. Vera is stung several times before she feels the twinges in her chest.

Thank You for the Music

Roger wipes down the barrel of his gun and picks up the bag of pheasants.

"Right," Colbear says, checking his watch and addressing his shooting party. "Back to the house, gentlemen, our entertainment will be waiting."

"What kind of entertainment have you got planned, Kevin?" Roger hears Peter Green say. He frowns at the man, he knows full well what kind of entertainment Colbear has organised, he'd put him in touch with them, indirectly. Green points back over the fields towards Colbear's farmhouse. Roger turns and sees the police car.

Tropical Loveland

Vera sits in her armchair and watches as a pair of blackbirds pick mealworms from a bird table in the garden. Roger was right, a change around of the living room did make the place feel brand new.
Sitting in the sunlight lifts her mood and she can't deny there isn't an enormous sense of relief now her mother is gone. Roger walks down the small pathway between the flowerbeds and the lawn, towards his shed, a spring in his step. When the ceiling came down, something inside her husband came down too. His walls. Vera's brush with death made him finally realise that he actually loved her, needed her, and could have lost her that evening three months before. Although her mother had died, along with the man who had been hiding in their attic, something had awoken in Roger. They started acting as they had done decades before.

Everyone was used to seeing Vera's familiar face on the high street and at her regular haunts but tongues soon started wagging when she had her handsome husband on her arm.
"I never realised these places were such a treasure trove," Roger says, as they tour the charity shops and jumble sales.
"What about all the kindling I brought home?" she says, all coy, like she used to act when they were courting.
"Pffff, God, I didn't half talk a load of bollocks."
"I suppose I did bring home a lot of junk."

"No, no, you didn't. Everyone's got a right to like what they want to. You've never begrudged me anything." It was in one of *her* shops that he'd found an archaic Guinness Book of Records, so old it was small and paperback with hardly any pictures.

Once he began collecting things, he couldn't stop. They would scout second-hand book shops, visiting new towns, and spending so much time together that everything came out of the woodwork. He'd changed that night when the paramedics rushed her into hospital, sat by her bedside holding her hand, which he had never done whilst she mourned the loss of her mother.

"I've never been one to show my emotions, it's just not the manly thing to do, is it? I'm sorry I mask it all with anger."

He had tears in his eyes and was nothing like the man she had married. Had he finally seen the error of his ways? When he actually cried, in front of the male doctor, Vera knew it was genuine. Her Roger would never do a thing like that. Never.

He felt bad for the way he had treated her, put it down to the stress of working, feeling inadequate for not being able to father a child, and eventually her mother's illness. He knew these things were inexcusable reasons for him to act the way he had for so long but he thought they had been given a second chance; her chest pain during the accident was nothing more than panic.

Vera laughs quietly as she looks up at the new living-room ceiling, it has been a nice couple of months. Like another honeymoon. No arguments. Roger paid top price for her mother's funeral and the newly renovated loft from his redundancy money without griping like the miser he once was. They go for Sunday lunch at The Crown every week and tea there on a Wednesday. The pub patrons were just as shocked as Roger to learn that the man in the attic had been a regular of theirs, John Farrington. She had never really spoken to the man, knew he'd worked with Roger at the factory years ago but had been sacked for theft before redundancy came. He had even attended their wedding; he was only a lad but she'd had a feeling about him even then. Everyone who'd ever known him said he was harmless, aside from that thing about his mother when he was a nipper, but he was forever committing acts of theft.

"It's my fault," said Roger. "I used to tell him how I was going to make loads of money from fixing stuff up. Probably thought all that crap I had stashed up there was worth something. There wasn't a lock he couldn't get through, the daft bugger. Reckon he thought there was a treasure trove up there and instead he got bees up his bum and a broken neck." They laughed sadly at that until tears came.

Dum Dum Diddle

The prepaid stamp on the envelope reads 'Willis and Sons Solicitors.'

Vera hears the toilet flush. *It's now or never.* She walks into the kitchen and waits for Roger to come out of the bathroom. He opens the door and jokingly clamps a hand to his chest. "Jesus, if I hadn't just been, you would've scared the crap out of me."

Vera crinkles her nose in disgust at the foul emissions coming from the bathroom.

"Sorry, love," Roger says, dipping back into the room to spray pine air freshener.

"Roger, it's okay, come here, please."

Her husband reappears, air freshener still in hand. "'ere, you don't fancy going on the 94 to that new buffet place, do you?"

Vera waves the envelope at him and sees the old greed ignite in his eyes. "Now, I want you to kno-"

He snatches the already open envelope and pulls out the letter. She sees his eyes gliding busily over the page before the hand holding it crumples the thick paper slightly. "The doddery old cunt..."

"Roger!"

"We can contest it," he says, his eyes burning into hers. "She wasn't of sound mind."

"Roger-"

All colour and emotion drain from him. She thinks he is about to have a stroke. When he looks at her again, the kitchen feels claustrophobic. The hatred in his eyes traps her in place.

"You cunt!" With one stride, he is across the room. He swings a fist into her face, cracking her glasses against the bridge of her nose. She spins around and smacks into the fridge door, scattering magnets — from destinations they have never visited — onto the floor as she falls.
"Cunt, cunt, cunt!" Roger screams, in tears, accentuating each word with a kick to her ribs.
The honeymoon is over.

Love Isn't Easy (But it Sure is Hard Enough)

They hate one another but she is too afraid of his fists to make her feelings known. Roger spends his time in his shed where he brews gut-rot concoctions and smokes until he can barely breathe.

It's the cigarettes that'll kill him, Vera thinks, although she secretly fantasises about having a hand in his demise. However, they will have both taken a great chunk out of their eighth decade before that happens.

It is a sunny afternoon, around three o'clock. Roger hasn't come in to grab a sandwich like he usually does, and she goes outside to sit on the bench in the sun.

Since Vera's mother died and left all her savings to the PDSA, Roger has found ways to punish her for her involvement in the will. He splurged their savings on getting her beloved garden paved over, hitting her where it hurt. By then, she had finally learned that the secret to beating her husband was to never, ever show that he had caused her pain.

 Smiling, she commented on how nice it looked, and how it would stop him traipsing mud in the house when he came in from the shed.

She promptly ordered a patio table and chairs and a large bird table.

Soon the bird table was accompanied by large terracotta flower pots and a wood burner, little things to make the space hers and piss Roger off at the same time.

She turned his act of spite into a peaceful spot for relaxation and reading. If she was still enough, the birds would come back and she could watch them like she used to. The tranquility of her place was often tainted by the background noise of Roger; when he knew she was outside, the volume on his radio would increase as would the profanities he shrieked at his latest losses on the football and horse races, but Vera had years of experience of blotting out her husband's mindless racket. It was why she misinterpreted his cries of pain for those of frustration and anger and carried on reading whilst he clutched at his bursting heart through his sweat-soaked vest mere feet away.

ABBA made her check on him.
Roger hated the Swedish pop group with an intensity bordering on psychotic. Although she was fond of their music, he had forbidden her to listen to it in his company as it set his teeth on edge. The irony that *Thank You For the Music* was the song playing whilst Roger was lying dead in the shed was lost on her. It didn't register until she took up humming through the second chorus and missed a few beats as her voice faltered.
He hadn't turned it off.
Roger hasn't turned ABBA off.
Darkness falls over her, although there isn't a cloud in the sky, it is more spiritual than visual and she feels cool in the afternoon sun. "Roger!" she calls, expecting some verbal abuse, part of her wanting it.
Nothing.
Vera puts down her book and tells herself he is probably asleep in that stinking armchair after too much of his homebrew, but she remembers his little outburst during the football results ten minutes before.

She hammers on the shed door, doesn't burst in; he used to keep dirty magazines in there and she has no desire to catch him doing anything disgusting. *No answer.*
 Steeling herself to be reprimanded for disturbing him, Vera opens the door timidly.
Roger sits in the armchair, slumped on one elbow, staring lifelessly at the rafters. One hand rests on his fat stomach just below his left breast, the other holds a slip of paper from the bookies. *This is not YOUR House. 25/1*
"Oh," Vera says, with numb indifference to the man she has been married to for decades. There is no sadness, only mild surprise and a hint of confusion, as though she is answering the door to an unexpected visitor.

The Winner Takes it All

Roger never really leaves her.

She feels him in the house almost every day. The memory of her husband lingers on like permanent stains that no amount of cleaning or redecoration can rid. Wafts of his black cherry tobacco — which she would always buy for him from the sweet shop — come and go like light summer breezes. Whenever she smells these things she feels *these* things: *Frightened. Insecure. Worthless. Old.* She knows it's her mind tricking her, that dead is dead, but it doesn't lessen the effects.

On days such as these, she barely eats, and sinks into a depression that wastes hours. It is his doing, albeit through her own conscience. But Vera is stubborn and powers through these dark days; whilst her body and mind allow, she tries her best to occupy herself with the things she loves.

Tuesdays and Fridays are her beacons in the storm. Tuesdays and Fridays are when Emilia comes around. Because Emilia never mentions anything untoward in the house, Vera understands it's all in her head. Guilt, most likely. Guilt about Roger breathing his last in the shed whilst she listened to ABBA and enjoyed a book in the sun.

Emilia is an angel: a petite, pale-skinned, blonde Polish elf, unofficial home help.

She pauses, vacuum in hand, finger poised as though she just remembered something. She bounds through a lounge she's just finished dusting. Vera loves how much vibrancy and energy is packed into someone so small. She watches as Emilia takes something from her bag.

"Before I forget," she says, and hands over a mauve envelope.

Vera's heart glows. She hates the way her fingers shake as she pulls the card from the envelope. "Oh, how lovely, Emilia, peonies," Vera says, admiring the floral watercolour below the birthday greeting. "Oh, let me get my readers, all I can make out is the big eighty-five."

"It's okay," says Emilia. "The greeting says 'Wszystkiego najlepszego z okazji urodzin.' It means 'Best wishes for a happy birthday now that you are eighty-five.'"

"Well, I still want my readers," Vera says, clutching the card to her breast as if it is her most treasured possession, and forages around on a small table beside her. She puts on spectacles and smiles at the card. "It's beautiful, Emilia, I've never had a Polish birthday card before, thank you."

Emilia returns Vera's gaze with the affection one would reserve for a beloved grandparent. "I remembered the discussion we had a while ago, how you say that you have always been interested in the world but never travelled. I see your books on your shelf each time I clean, about different countries and their cultures, so I get you this." Emilia takes a book out from behind her back and hands it to Vera.

Vera feels tears in her eyes as she takes the book from the beautiful Polish girl. It is a heavy hardback, an illustrated guidebook to her home country. "Oh, Emilia, I don't know what to say." Vera gives into her building emotions and holds her arms open. "Come here."

Emilia crouches down and puts her arms around Vera. "You are a remarkable woman, Vera. I never knew my grandmother but I hope she was like you."

Vera pulls away from her and grins when she sees that Emilia, too, is crying. "Look at the pair of us! Daft clots!"

Vera pecks her on the cheek and hands her the book. "Be a love and put it pride of place on the mantelpiece, please, the card too. I shall read that with my pot of tea at three." Emilia takes great care in making room amongst the delicate ornamental menagerie above the electric fire.

"You know, Roger, my husband, used to hate my books on other countries."

"How so?"

"He was a racist bastard!" Vera snaps, and chuckles at Emilia's open-mouth.

"There's no other word for him! Bastard, that's what he was. A racist, sexist, lying, swindling bastard. God curse his stinking, rotting soul."

"Whoa!" Emilia says, startled but blatantly impressed. "He sounds like a lot of the men and women I know."

Vera shakes her head in disgust. "I've never understood it."

"Men?"

Vera laughs, "No, racism. Mind you, I've never understood men, either. I've always been interested in different things than them."

Emilia already knows this. Vera's old house was a wonderland of curios from around the world. Ornaments and draperies, trinkets and talismanic emblems. A whole world of souvenirs. Complete tat to some, but a treasure trove to Vera. And yet she had never set foot off English soil. "Why haven't you travelled?" Emilia pauses. "I mean, after, Roger passed away."

"Oh, travelling is a young person's game. I was too old then."

"But you have the money to do it in style."

A spark of youthful excitement ignites in Vera's eyes but it is only momentary. "Oh, I can barely walk unaided nowadays."

Emilia places the book on the mantelpiece and stands the card beside it. "I could come with you, I have savings."

"You'd do that for me?" Vera squeaks, close to tears again.

"You have said yourself that being stuck in this house gets you down. So, get out. Even if it's only for a holiday."

"A holiday?"

"Two weeks!"

"Oh, well, I never..."

"Anywhere in the world!"

"Anywhere?"

"Anywhere!"

Vera is astonished by the fact she is seriously considering it. Her last holiday must have been at least fifteen years before Roger died, and that had been a wet weekend in Blackton, most of which he'd spent in the pub while she'd spent her time in the B&B eating chocolate and reading. Could they do it? She trusts Emilia; the girl has been coming in three times a week for six years and has never taken anything off her. The idea that she would spend her savings to take a silly old bat anywhere in the world, though, that wasn't on. Vera thinks about the day Roger died, the heart attack, and the piece of paper that had caused it. He had won big, big money on the horses and the shock had killed him outright. She didn't even find out until the day after he died and went through his stuff. *This is not YOUR House* had come in first; she never has understood the racing odds. The newspapers wanted to make a big song and dance about it but she refused to be named or photographed. They labelled her a 'grieving widow.' The papers always lied, she thought the irony was hilarious and that it served the old bastard right. *Finally, he gets what he wants and then bang, he's dead.*

Our Last Summer

Vera has felt ill since getting up this morning. There is nothing specific she can pinpoint or aim painkillers at, just an all-around feeling of sickness. It niggles at her and tells her to get out of bed half an hour before her usual time, and it bemoans like an unsatisfied teenager when she finally rises.

Her appetite isn't much to speak of anymore, she usually has a vague interest for tea and toast first thing, but even forcing that down is a chore today.

At eighty-five, she is no stranger to a doctor's surgery, however, she hates them with a passion usually reserved for Jehovah's Witnesses and tin openers. She is adamant that she will only bother her GP if she feels it is something serious, and this feeling of general deflation does not fit into that category.

No, she is made of stronger stuff than that, raised in the age where people were taught to fight, to grin and bear it. And not too deep inside her, there is an intense fear that this time it would be the start of something. Something that will lead her down death's narrow pathway.

The thought of death frightens her. When she was young, all the old folk seemed to have a peaceful indifference when they would speak about their deaths, but she has always been petrified at the thought of her own. It hasn't lessened with age.

"It's old age, daft old bat." She says it out loud. She often speaks her thoughts, sometimes it is the only voice she hears for days on end. *Old age and excitement, perhaps,* she thinks, as she considers eyeing the Poland book standing on the mantelpiece.

It has been there a few weeks now and she has already devoured it twice over.

After much deliberation, Emilia has succumbed to Vera's offer of paying for her to accompany her on her first — and probably only — foreign holiday. The two weeks have been bumped up to four and they will be visiting almost every country in the whole of Europe, including Emilia's homeland. Vera's usual Wednesday trip to the town centre will involve one irregular activity. Whilst picking up her pension from the post office, she will also get a passport application form, which Emilia will help her complete the next day.

She makes the necessary preparations, hooks her walking stick over the handle of her shopping trolley, and leaves the house for the quarter-past nine bus.

The heat hits her as soon as she gets outside and she curses herself for not having checked the weather forecast. She stops and glances at her watch to see if she has the time to go back for her sun hat. No such luck. There is no way she is going to wait an hour for another bus so she continues towards the stop.

A young man sits on the top of the bus shelter bench in the haphazard fashion that youngsters do. Vera keeps her eye on him: the main road is straight for at least two miles, if he stands up she will know the bus is in sight. She always panics, even though she gives herself plenty of time to allow for mishaps.

When she gets close to the shelter she smiles a greeting to the youth, an instinctive reaction, and tries not to crinkle her nose at the funny smell coming from his roll-up. "It's a hot one today, isn't it?"

The lad throws the butt of his roll-up on the ground and lets it smoulder. "Yeah," he says, nodding at her from beneath the brim of his baseball cap.

Vera nods and moves into the shelter to sit beside him. The smell from his cigarette is now combined with the stench of way too much aftershave or deodorant and it makes her feel queasy, but to move now will look impolite. She straightens and looks through the Plexiglas for any sign of the oncoming bus. Her eyesight is shocking. She places a hand gently on the boy's forearm. "I say, young man, could you let me know when you see the bus coming as it takes me a while to get up and I'm rubbish at seeing things far away."

"Yeah, yeah, sure. Should be here in a minute," he says, pulling his arm away. Vera notices symbols tattooed on fair, freckled skin with fine ginger hairs. Her close-up vision is perfect. "Oh, that's an interesting tattoo. Is it Japanese?"

The boy rubs a hand over the symbols as though they will come off if people mention them. A nervous thing, no doubt. "Yeah. It means 'fearless.'"

"Oh, I see," Vera says, noticing that for someone so fearless, he is avoiding eye contact. "How lovely. Maybe I should get a tattoo. What would you recommend?"

He grins down at her and Vera notices he is quite a handsome chap beneath the hat. Well-defined features and startling blue eyes that you can't help but stare at a bit too long. "Maybe some flowers."

"I do like my flowers. Does it hurt?"

The boy's head darts in the opposite direction and back at her. "Bus is coming."

"Oh." Vera braces herself on her trolley and pushes herself up. She squints up the road into the distance and can make out a red square gradually coming into focus. She opens her handbag and takes out her pass as the bus pulls into the layby. "Well, it was jolly nice to talk to you, and maybe I'll get that tattoo," she says, gesturing for the boy to get on first.

"Nah, you go first, it's alright."

"Age before beauty, as they say. Thank you so much," Vera says, stepping up, smiling at the driver, scanning her pass and finding the nearest seat, grateful for the young man's conversation and the momentary distraction from the heat.

The air conditioning is a blessed relief, the café is always her first destination once she reaches town. A young couple are sitting at her usual table by the window, she smiles at them as she wheels her trolley past. It is nice to see some younger people in the café rather than the same old fuddy-duddies.

"Morning, Vera," a tall lady with long black plaits calls across from the cash register as a man in a straw hat pays his bill.

"Hello, Chantal," Vera says, and suddenly stops as a wave of dizziness runs up her spine and neck and over her head, making her scalp crawl. Her vision doubles, the muscles of her eyes beyond her control, and she thinks she might vomit.

The young couple must have seen her falter; the man jumps to her aid and puts his arm around her, his partner by his side.

Their concerned sentiments are drowned out by the blood rushing in her ears, but Vera allows herself to be steered to a seat. Everything swims for a few seconds before Chantal's face hovers before hers and things settle.

"Oh," Vera says, feeling the first waves of embarrassment pinch at her cheeks. She feels her bladder leak a little; fear of public embarrassment is worse than the funny turn — and what it could mean.

"Vera, are you okay?"

"I think the heat's got to me," she says, offering a faint smile, partly to check that her facial muscles haven't atrophied. She feels sick, weak, and hot.

"Have you eaten today? Drunk anything other than tea?" Chantal says, like a stern daughter.

"Oh, well, you know, me and my appetite."

"Right, you sit here and I'm going to get you a glass of water and then you can look at the dessert menu and we'll see about a pot of tea. You really should think about what I said about switching to decaf..."

"Oh, I don't know about these new-fangled things, Chantal."

Chantal rolls her eyes and grins at the young couple.

"Would you mind if Vera joins you guys? It's right by the door and cooler..."

"Oh, I don't want to intrude on the young lovebirds," Vera protests.

"It's fine," the woman says, and the man agrees.

"You'll do as you're told in my café, Vera," Chantal says, with a wink to the young couple to reassure them that she has her best interests at heart. "This is Michael and Ginelle, they'll look after you."

Vera begins to feel a little better after the water and a scone, but when she opens up her handbag to pay the bill the nausea comes back, with chest pains this time.

"My purse has gone." There is no doubt about it; the thing was the size of a brick.

She catches the sympathetic expression Chantal throws to the young couple before smiling down at her. "Oh dear, Vera. Do you think maybe you might have left it at home?"

"No." Vera takes a deep breath, and that is when the chest pains resume and the queasy feeling returns. "I never leave home without it. It stays in my bag." She ignores the chest pains; they are only dull anyway. She can't have dropped it; she hasn't even needed to touch it yet. Her bus pass was kept separately.

"I think I'm going to be sick." Vera snatches a napkin from the table. She doesn't hurl but the dizziness overwhelms her and she feels herself slip from the chair and onto the tiled floor.

"Vera!" Chantal shouts, and kneels beside her.

Vera pulls herself up to a sitting position using the chair. "I really don't feel very well."

"Right, that's it," Chantal says, and helps her back to the chair. "I'm taking you over to the walk-in centre right now."

Vera nods, and without any fight allows herself to be led to the NHS walk-in centre on the opposite side of the High Street.

"Right," Chantal says, stepping away from the reception desk. "Rose here will phone me when you are finished, and I'll get someone to cover me and I'll take you home or wherever you need to go, okay?"

Wherever you need to go. Vera does not like the sound of that at all. The chest pain is likely to be indigestion from being forced to eat on a hot day, and the other symptoms are probably signs of a bit of heatstroke. She opens her mouth to protest, but the café waitress knows her better than she knows herself.

"Don't you try and argue with me or Rose here will tell you off!" Chantal says, and walks to the water cooler and back, not giving her a chance to utter a word. "Just chill out and do as you're told."

Vera nods, takes the water, and watches Chantal leave. She hates old age.

For how many years have people treated her like an old person? Spoken to her in special voices that are reserved only for the young and the decrepit?

Infantile, that's how the younger people see her; she remembers thinking the same about her mother.

When had her own voice changed in conversation with her mum? When her Alzheimer's became too severe?

Old age is cruel, a thief, a family friend or relative, someone that's always been there in the background and then you find out they've been stealing from you for decades. Sometimes it creeps up like a stealthy cat-burglar, biding its time, choosing what to take, before pouncing and taking everything all at once.

A tall figure walks past her and bends over the reception desk and she catches a familiar smell. This rings alarm bells in her head.

"Excuse me, darling, how much longer have I got to wait? Been sitting here hours."

The receptionist taps at a keyboard. "Shouldn't be long now, sir."

"Fuck's sake!" The hunched-over figure slams his palms against the desk and stands up. When he turns around to survey the crowded waiting room, he takes off his baseball cap and runs a hand over his sweaty bald head. It's the kid from the bus stop. "There's been people come in after me who've been seen already."

"Sir, we have to prioritise if there are emergencies," the receptionist says, catching the eye of a security guard.

"Ain't no fucking emergencies in here!" The kid scowls at the people waiting. He points at a little girl playing on her GameBoy. "How about her? She's fucking playing computer games!"

"Sir," says the security guard, bounding across the room, "if you don't stop using bad language we will have to ask you to leave. Please sit." All eyes are on the young man. Vera wonders what has instilled such anger in the young man, he didn't seem so bad at the bus stop. The muscles in his neck and jaw bunch as he sizes up the security guard, the tension building is exactly like something from one of her soaps.

"Hello again," Vera says sweetly, in a bid to defuse the situation. The man looks at her but she sees no recognition in his eyes, he ignores her and sits back down. The people sitting each side of him move to the edges of their seats. Vera watches as he sits with his head between his knees, rocking slightly.

She feels sorry for him, maybe he has some sort of mental trauma and isn't comfortable in these places; she can't blame him, she loathes them.

His hands bunch and unbunch, making the Japanese symbols on his forearm dance.

"I think I'll get roses," Vera says, "for my flower tattoo."

Slowly, he raises his eyes to her; there is no mistaking those eyes. "I don't know what the fuck you're on about, love," he spits coldly.

The words sting, and talking only seems to agitate him. He begins to swear under his breath. A nurse appears from a door beside the reception desk and everyone gives her their attention. When the nurse says someone else's name, he jumps to his feet.

"Oi!" he says, directing his anger towards the nurse who is in the process of leading an elderly Indian couple towards the practitioners' rooms. "They've only been in here ten fucking minutes!"

"I'm sorry, sir," the nurse begins, clearly agitated.

"Right, you. Out, now!" The security guard steps forward and points toward the door.

The man sneers at the guard; the nurse and the elderly couple are a picture of confusion and fear. Even if they can't understand the verbal language, they can understand the body.

"That's it, all you fucking Pakis stick together!"

"You mustn't say stuff like that!" Vera finds herself scolding him like a child and the urge to stand up and slap his face temporarily overrides her ill feelings.

"Fuck off and mind your own business, you old cunt!"

The security guard reaches for the man's left arm but his right shoots out. His fist connects with the guard's eye and sends him face-first into the wall.

Vera is livid. She has had enough violence in her life. She thrusts her shopping trolley forward into the back of the young man's legs; it rolls forward freely. It barely jostles him but it gets his attention.

"Stop showing off, you bloody idiot!" He turns around, face red with rage, and before he can decorate the air with another garland of obscenities she cuts him off. She stands up on doddery legs to retrieve her trolley. "Look at you, acting like the big man now you've got an audience. Why don't you tell everyone here how much of a gentleman you really are? Blushing when spoken to. Helping little old ladies onto buses."

His manic grin turns into one of amusement and finally recognition. He remembers her. Behind him, the guard gets to his feet and tells the receptionist to call the police. The man leans in close to Vera, his horrid, sweet odour engulfing her. He speaks only loud enough for her to hear. "It's amazing how gentlemanly I can be when I'm trying to snatch an old cunt's purse, isn't it?" With that, he puts both hands on her shoulders, shoves her back towards the seats, and runs from the building.

Despite the pain of landing hard on the uncomfortable chair, despite still feeling more ill than she has in a long, long time, Vera musters up enough energy to grab her trolley and walk outside to the taxi rank. An emergency ten-pound note tucked into her bus pass gets her home.

Vera feels the oppression of the house as she stands in the gateway, the windows bulging with malevolence. It is typical *he* would be here this afternoon.

The heat was so intense in the taxi that she had to swallow back vomit most of the ride home, and now, as the sun scorches her, it comes out relentlessly. Vera stumbles against her trolley as thin gruel spills over her chin. She finds her house keys and leaves the trolley on the grass.

She can smell him when she enters the house: black cherry tobacco, and this time something else, too. She understands it is in her head, like the ill feelings that always coincide with these smells. Her gorge rises once more as the foreign, yet somehow familiar odour registers with her olfactory senses.

It's the bitter tang of her dead husband's sweaty vests. It's exactly what that disgusting armchair smelt like, the one that sat in his shed for years and moulded to his shape. The one that he died in. If it was possible to bottle the essence of the bastard, it would smell exactly like this.

She picks up the phone and speed-dials Emilia, cancelling her visit that afternoon, telling her about the incident with the tattooed, supposedly fearless man, insisting that she is fine and that she will contact the police immediately.

She's being stupid, she knows that, there's no such thing as ghosts, really; living, breathing people are far worse than anything make-believe and that's exactly why so many people seek solace in fiction, or the wonderful world of the supernatural.

A cup of tea will put you right. Her mother's cure-all. Vera pushes herself up out of the armchair but a hot wave of dizziness and nausea forces her back onto the cushions. Her chest is heavy, something is seriously wrong. She grabs the cordless phone off the table and lets gravity claim her. The stench of Roger engulfs her then, stifling and suffocating. Vera props herself up against the cushion of the armchair and presses the speed dial options.

Who will get here faster: Emilia, or an ambulance?

A pain in her chest incapacitates her and the wrist of the hand holding the phone feels like it is being grasped by an invisible force. The handset falls from her grasp and the pain inside her surpasses anything she has ever experienced.

Vera falls back onto the floor. A rustling in her line of vision captures her attention and it will be the last thing she ever sees. The cover to Emilia's book on Poland crumples and tears, crushed by an invisible hand, just like Vera's heart.

Transition

The Day Before You Came

There's a funny little man in the corner of Neil's bedroom; a man who wasn't there a second ago. He seemed to flutter out from beneath the loose piece of wallpaper by the radiator as though he were made of plaster dust. Neil grabs on to the bars of his cot and pulls himself up. He's filled with excitement and warmth; someone has come to see him in the middle of the night. The man is old, has a wobbly face, hair like cobwebs, and wears old brown clothes, but has the biggest smile he has ever seen. Neil reaches out a chubby hand and when the man touches him it's like the cold air that comes in through the letterbox. He's friendly, the old man, and always so, so happy. He calls Neil *Neilly-Wheelie* and that always makes them both laugh. It isn't until Neil is a few months older and stringing more coherent words together that Neil says this nickname in reference to himself whilst playing with his mum, and Mummy does *that* face where it seems she's going to cry.

Neilly-Wheelie is the name her dad had given Neil when he was just two weeks old. Her dad died soon after.

I've Been Waiting for You

Neil sits with Philippa because nobody else likes him. Nobody really likes Philippa, either. Neil knows why the other boys and girls don't like him but doesn't understand why they don't like her. Philippa is a lovely girl with hair the colour of conkers and which always smells like fresh apples or honey. To begin with, they sit together in silence, both children downtrodden before they've had a chance to rise amongst their peers. The other children call Philippa fat but Neil doesn't look at people the same way others do. When he looks at the girl he sits beside in class, he sees someone beautiful who glows with a secret light that only special people like him can see. Most of the time this light is subdued, sunlight on a hazy day, but once they start talking to each other he sees such vibrancy that he has to look away. His own light is a watercolour of mauves and violets, transparent as though dispersed by raindrops.

"The others think I'm a weirdo," he tells her, tucking long black hair behind his ears. "I don't like playing with the other boys anyway."

"I thought you were a little girl when I first saw you," Philippa admits.

Neil nods, smiling, thinks things would be a lot easier if he were a little girl. "I'm scared of the hairdressers."

"It don't hurt," she says, twiddling with her own brown locks.

"It might hurt *me*," he answers, and she doesn't argue like all the others.

They read, they walk, they talk. They endure their battles together and eventually learn to shield one another from the arrows.

The Day Before You Came

From a Twinkling Star to a Passing Angel

Neil realises they're ghosts when he sees Mrs. Howes three weeks after the headmaster told everyone she'd died.

Mrs. Howes was the music teacher, a skinny, witchy woman with wild grey hair and big yellow teeth. Despite being so scary looking, she had been a nice old lady and could play on the piano any song you could think of. They would have music lessons, all sat cross-legged on the cold assembly hall floor, and she would perch on her stool at the gleaming piano, fingers blurring, as she taught them songs for their upcoming performances. They would take it in turns to sit beside her and she would teach them to play simple songs, nursery rhymes. She was surrounded by wafts of furniture polish and leather and her aura burned with Autumnal colours.

Neil was upset when he heard about Mrs. Howes's death, he even cried when he was alone, but some of the other boys and girls didn't care at all. Some even laughed.

He sees her again when he's crossing the hall to the office after their teacher has taken the register. First of all he feels the swish of something invisible pass him, and smells the familiar aromas of polish and leather. The footsteps become audible, as though someone is slowly increasing the volume, then Mrs. Howes appears, becoming more tangible the closer she gets to her cherished piano. Neil freezes; he's never seen them appear, they're usually just there and then they're not. Now he realises that this is an actual ghost, fear begins to twinkle inside his chest — but it's nothing compared to how he feels when the other boys are teasing him in the playground.

Mrs. Howes settles at the piano but instead of music, like Neil is expecting, soft, hitching sobs are the only sounds that fill the hall. Neil looks on from afar, notices that the autumn fire that surrounded her whilst she was alive has gone. No, not gone, changed, as if the light is now the only part of her that remains, her leftovers, and have shaped the person she was when she was alive. Neil is heartbroken that she's sad, and wants to help. He's not spoken to any of these special people since he was very little, when his grandfather used to visit him, and even though he is scared, the urge to help overrides the fear. Neil thinks Mrs. Howes is crying because the cover to the piano keys is down but it's because she can't touch the piano at all. With each wracking sob she becomes more transparent and the burning oranges fade beneath her ethereal skin. Neil puts down the register, lifts the lid, and plays the only song he knows all the way through. A song Mrs. Howes had taught him: Twinkle, Twinkle, Little Star, and then Mrs. Howes stops crying, smiles, and explodes with all the colours of bonfire night. She's October personified.

SOS

Neil's fear of the things he sees weakens as he grows; he's learned, at too young an age, that it's the living who we have to be truly frightened of. The colours he sees around people, colours that are invisible to most of us, he understands are an extension of their personality. He hasn't learned the word *aura* yet. The ghosts are the person's after-image, their leftovers, whatever remains after they've left this world physically. The leftovers mostly keep themselves to themselves. Some like to relive their favourite pastimes, some go about generic daily chores in a replay of normal, mundane, key points in their lives. Rarely does he see any that are sad (or at least seem to be sad) and rarely do they acknowledge him. It's as though their realm and his are two different films projected onto the same cinema screen. He doesn't experience any bad leftovers until he goes to his best friend Philippa's house for the second time.

Most buildings, Neil notices, have their own special feeling about them. Whether it's because they're old and have had as many families as paint layers within their walls, or because they are new and raised upon the grounds of something steeped in rich history. Once, when he was on holiday with his mum, they had gone into a supermarket and there were a few leftovers lingering about in old-fashioned clothes, holding artists' paintbrushes. Neil didn't say anything, didn't discover the newly erected supermarket was on the site where an art college used to be, but merely accepted it for what it was.

Buildings, over the years, he has learned, absorb emotions

as paint absorbs nicotine. They yellow with the strongest scenes and interactions that happened within them, and sometimes, if a person is sensitive enough, they can be picked up on.

When he goes to Philippa's house, he's intrigued from the get-go. He's never seen a house so narrow and so tall. The three-storey town house is old, too, and the first surprise is the absence of any feeling when he gets in there. Usually, the older places set his skin a-tingling. After this initial revelation, Neil does what he always does: he accepts the situation and moves on, excited by the prospect of spending time with his friend.

Philippa's room is right up in the roof and they race up and down the stairs with an energy they've never seemed to be able to muster up at school. Philippa's parents are easy-going, funny, and warm. They are happy their daughter has such a devoted, well-mannered friend and not once, (unlike most of the other adults, especially the teachers) have they mentioned the length of his hair. They let the children be themselves and the first time at Philippa's is a treat which Neil never wants to end. There is food, there is fun, and there is no prejudice.

He soon forgets the blank atmosphere; he's only young, so perhaps such places do exist after all.

When he returns to Philippa's, it's as if the house was holding its breath before. As soon as he crosses the threshold, darkness bleeds in around his peripheral vision. The corners and shadows are alive with some unseen, glowering malignancy. Neil can't understand what it is, but the whole place feels bad, ruined, as though something terrible has happened deep within the building's history, and the stains, whether visible or not, are indelible. Fear knots his insides, and imaginary spectres, not leftovers, peek at him from behind every door. Eyes follow him wherever he is but there is nothing to see, nothing to hear. His skin is alive with the supernatural electricity of the place and he has to get out. Philippa finds Neil in the garden where he stares at the windows waiting for the leftovers to show themselves, convinced there must be some here, to explain why the house feels the way it does. He can't hide his anguish from his best friend, and even though it might cost him his only companion, he divulges everything, tells her all about the leftovers. Ghosts and auras and atmospheric changes.

Philippa listens and doesn't judge; her secret colours fade a little but the glowing sunlight that surrounds her still burns closely to her skin. She tells him that a man and a woman had a fight in her house, years ago, and the man died. It's the missing jigsaw piece in the mystery of Philippa's house. Neil senses the sadness, regret and bitterness within the building and knows with certainty that the man didn't die of natural causes.

They go back into the building and Neil tries to pass on a message to the man, to his leftover, if it's still hanging around. It's okay, *she's* not here. There's no need to be frightened anymore.

The next time they're at Philippa's, the house has changed once again. He detects the change, but it's subtle, as if the unseen presence has summoned the courage to trust, to be themselves, now they know there's no danger here.

Arrival

Neil has never thought of himself as a boy. Gender never comes into the equation when he thinks about himself but as he grows alongside Philippa he discovers that he wants to be more like her. She is brave and strong and rises above the continuous torments about her weight. She is beautiful, and, at first, he questions whether he's in love with her, but it's not long before he realises he wants to be like her. A woman. Once Neil has had this revelation he is overcome with joy, he could take off with it, rise up into the sky and blind even the unbelievers with the brightness of his aura. This worm has finally discovered that it's a caterpillar and there is nothing wrong with wanting to be the butterfly.

The Day Before You Came

As Good as New

Things are difficult once Neil decides to emerge. The first people he tells are his mum and Philippa. His mum is shocked, worried he will get into something he'll regret, but she knows nothing about this kind of thing, doesn't understand that it will make absolutely no difference to her. He takes the first step in his transition when he leaves school. Neil is now Niamh (pronounced 'Neema' mostly to take the attention away from anything else people might ask) and living as the opposite gender to what he was assigned at birth. It's hardly anything to be noticed physically, her clothes stay the same, as well as her mannerisms, and it will be years before operations are even considered, but to her, it's everything.

Being Niamh unleashes the full potential that was hidden within, the colours that surrounded her as Neil are fuller now, and spread as though the butterfly really has arrived.

Niamh's confidence is emboldened by this sudden release and she embraces who she is at last, unafraid of the things she sees and the things she wants to do.

The leftovers are as frequent as ever; she sees them everywhere but she'd learned at a very young age who she could talk to about such things. Philippa doesn't believe in the supernatural but she believes in her friend, and has the decency to accept when there are places she's uncomfortable in.

Part 2:

Another Town, Another Train

Why Did It Have to Be Me?

Philippa isn't a stranger to six a.m, and besides, it is nice being awake early, before everything kicks off. Her parents are early-risers for work, consistently eager to rush to their jobs as though they could toil away the last few years before retirement in record time if only they tried harder. It isn't until she gets outside after just enough water to moisten her mouth and throat that she revels in the morning.

She never bothers with stretching before runs, or does much in the way of warming up unless there are any aches or pains hanging over from the previous day. She simply gets her running kit on, switches on all necessary apps to track and trace, and gets going. There is no better thing to wake her up; caffeine does nothing much for her other than elevate her heart rate and make her more tired. Her best friend, Niamh, taught her that exercise first thing sets you up for the day. Every time she runs, she says a secret prayer of thanks for her friend. She owes her pretty much everything. Seven years earlier she was a size 22, could barely walk two miles without collapsing in a hot, blubbery heap, and after a decade of intense bullying and victimisation masked as education, she tried to take her own life with a bunch of paracetamol. Niamh had always been her only friend, throughout both primary and secondary schools. They were a mismatched pair: Niamh petite, Philippa big and broad, and that gave the other kids more fuel. Philippa never recognised her own importance and value until she saw the hurt on Niamh's face when she found out she had attempted suicide. She needed Niamh, but until that moment, Philippa had never realised that Niamh needed her, too. Philippa knew Niamh had her own things to deal with but she came across as a pillar of strength. When confronted, Philippa admitted she hated herself, hated the way she looked and felt, and Niamh, ever the problem solver, solved the problem. Together they devised exercise routines and nutrition plans and Niamh became Philippa's personal trainer, something she was seeking as a vocation alongside being a nutritionist.

Niamh changed her life, saved her life, and even though it was so hard, it was really so easy.

Now she is thirty-four and her size-ten figure bolts alongside early morning commuters who puff cigarette smoke out of their car windows and shout the occasional lewd remark about the firmness of her arse and she smiles as she gives them the finger. *Ten kilometres, coffee, banana,* then *get ready for the viewing.*

The Visitors

When the bus pulls away, Philippa spots the house immediately. A little red car sits outside it, a few feet away from a bus shelter. Insignia on its side tells her it is the estate agent's. One of the key selling points for her was the proximity to a major bus route, it was a must for work. She tries to get a closer look at the bungalow's front garden whilst she waits at a set of traffic lights, but an overgrown hedge obscures most of it. As she approaches the house, a grey-haired woman gets out of the car.

The house isn't as empty as she'd expected; a three-piece suite fills the living room.
"Because you mentioned this was going to be your first home, I thought I'd give you first refusal on this suite." The estate agent waves a hand toward the furniture. "The previous tenant left all of her stuff to charity, but unfortunately none of the local ones had the facilities to remove this." She pauses, gauging Philippa's reaction. "I can get someone to take it away if you don't want it." Philippa inspects the sofa, which looks expensive and hardly used. It isn't something she would pick herself, but if she chooses to keep it, it would save a decent chunk of her finances. "Oh wow, yes. I'll keep it. I mean, thank you."
The agent smiles. "I remember when I was starting out, you need to save every penny you can."
"That's true." Philippa instantly likes the letting agent. She is down to earth and cool-looking. Her grey hair is pixie-cut in a punkish style that hints at possible wayward younger years, and she reminds her of a really cool form teacher from high school.

She lets herself be shown around the two-bedroom bungalow only half-listening to the technical details as the agent weaves about the building. "The living room ceiling, roof, and attic were replaced and renovated about fifteen years ago, after the people who owned it discovered a massive wasps' nest."

Philippa grimaces, and it doesn't go unnoticed.

"It's all gone and sealed up now, don't worry. When the old lady who owned it passed away we resurfaced the patio in the back garden and put in a lawn to break up the monotony, she requested and paid for it in her will. Weird, huh? So you'll be the first one to use that new area."

Philippa smiles enthusiastically but can't help but feel the sadness behind the lady's parting gesture. "I would have thought an old lady would have had some flower borders and such whilst she was alive, or is that something else that doesn't happen anymore?"

"I know, right? It was just one big concrete slab, like a car park. Maybe she didn't have green fingers."

"Maybe she buried her husband out there," Philippa says without thinking, and laughs with embarrassment. "I'm sorry."

The agent sees the funny side, however. "I'm just happy that you aren't put off by the fact somebody died in the house."

"I'm not worried about such things. I believe there's an explanation for everything."

"Good for you. I have to say, that sort of stuff gives me the willies. Although, saying that, I've never come across anything untoward in any of the properties I've shown."

"I have a friend who thinks she's a psychic, who thinks she can detect stuff everywhere, but even when she's said there were spirits in my parents' house, I never saw anything. It's not something I believe in." She is not one to 'pick up vibes about a place,' as Niamh puts it, all that is needed here aside from redecoration is a good clean and air to rid the house of the tobacco smell.

The agent pulls out some documents and places them onto the kitchen counter. "Well, I can see there are no flies on you. Right, if you sign here, I can get you the keys on Thursday."

I've Been Waiting For You

Philippa selects 'My Soundtrack' on Amazon Music, hooks the little cube-shaped Bluetooth speaker on a nail on the wall, and surveys the room. She rakes her red hair with her fingers and ties it back as she decides where to start.

"Yeah, bitch," she says, firing her index finger at the speaker as her favourite song by *Tones and I* comes on. She rips open a pack of paintbrushes and cracks a tin of paint with a flathead screwdriver. As the Australian singer screeches her way into the first chorus of Dance Monkey, Philippa wiggles her butt in time to the tune and slaps blood-red paint up and down the living room walls. "Dance for me, dance for me, dance for me, oh oh...oh, for fuck's sake!"

An intense waft of tobacco insults her nose and she puts down her brush. "Jesus, woman," she says, talking to the woman who died there, or at least her memory. "How the fucking hell did you make it to old age smoking like a chimney?" She opens a window and regrets not having followed her father's advice on stripping paint from the walls first; she has obviously disturbed nicotine ingrained into the paintwork. The cool air from outside soon dispels the unwanted odour and she makes a mental note to buy incense next time she goes to town. The room will look awesome once it is decked out in red and black. She has all of her additional furniture on order and she can't wait. At thirty-four she has finally got her *own* place and is starting her *own* life, at least that's what it feels like. Something she actually owns. She feels like a proper adult now, what with all the decorating and shit. Her parents always encouraged her independence and stubbornness, her determination to do everything herself. They recognised that she was a strong-willed woman who knew what she wanted, understood how important it was for her to use her own money that she had earned in her own job, which she had acquired with her own qualifications. She knew she could rely on them in times of need, but she would have to be down to her last penny to even consider that. Now they were both close to early retirement, she wanted them to relax and enjoy life again, without the responsibility of children, and to be able to make them proud. Ultimately, in their later years, she hoped to be able to spoil them as they had done her, growing up.

Philippa has forbidden them from even visiting the house until the time is right. She shall finish all the decorating, make it hers, and then unveil her pride and joy once it is complete. About the only thing she doubts she will achieve in the foreseeable future is giving them the grandchildren they secretly hope for. Most of her relationships have been with utter imbeciles; it appears she has an uncanny knack for inadvertently sniffing them out.

"Fuck men!" Philippa shouts over the music, and paints a huge, crude penis on the wall in red before slashing it with a big defiant 'X.' The breeze coming in means that almost all of the tobacco smell has gone. She makes yet another mental note to buy incense, citronella if possible, it has a great smell and keeps the bugs away. After adding a few more swathes of paint, a familiar song comes on and she thumbs up the volume on the speaker hanging on the nail. She slaps crimson streaks across the bare walls in time to the beat and basks in the memories the golden oldie brings. Dancing with her mum and dad at the holiday camp disco when she was little, before they went on their few exotic holidays. Glitterballs, colourful lights, sticky floors. All the mums would gravitate towards the dance floor when ABBA's Dancing Queen came on. Happy memories, good times.

"...for a dance," she sings as she brushes along to the music, swinging her hips, temporarily lost in time, somewhere back in the late 90s. "And when you get the chance — " a sudden wet glug, the music muffles and goes silent. Perplexed, Philippa looks at the space where the Bluetooth speaker had been hanging, and the hole where the nail had been. She looks down just in time to see the hanging thread of the speaker sink into the thick paint. "Disconnected," announces a small voice from the phone in her pocket.

"No, fucking, shit, Sherlock." Philippa bends to pick up the nail which lies on the bare floorboards and when she rights herself a waft of tobacco and unwashed armpits catches her off-guard. "Jesus Christ, woman," she says, still talking to the memory of the previous tenant. *Fuck it.* She decides to follow her father's advice and hire someone to strip the older layers of paint from the walls. It will take a wedge out of her savings but there is no way she can live with that foul smell; the tobacco is bad enough but the stale sweat that accompanied it just then was too much.

Little Things

She knows she is too trusting, that's why she's made sure to have her dad with her when they come around.
Although she didn't want to show her folks the new place before she'd made it her own, he won't pry or get under her feet.
The ad has been in the newsagent's window: a list of odd jobs, decorating prowess, above a name and number. If the guy is kosher, then it will be cheaper than hiring a professional, as long as it gets the job done.
The bloke turns up at the time he said he would, and has a paint stripper; he wasn't bad looking, either. Lean, muscular, and a bit rough around the edges, with a few DIY tattoos, not really her type but there is something about him, or maybe something about her that means she finds him appealing. He introduces himself as Ryan but the friend he's brought along to help out called him something else.
Philippa makes them drinks and listens as Ryan tells them about doing an apprenticeship in painting and decorating. Her dad seems to approve of his handiwork and banter.
It takes only a couple of days for them to strip all the walls, and despite Ryan offering her numerous deals, Philippa refuses his offer of decorating for her, but accepts the offer of meeting with him for a drink sometime.

Merry-go-round

"Entitled pricks, that's all they fucking are. Living off Mummy and Daddy's fortune." Ranga upends the can and teases out the last drops of strong lager. He tosses the empty over his shoulder into the street, amongst the kerbside refuse sacks from the nearby takeaways.
"Like that bird you're thinking about shagging?"
"Nah, you can tell her old man's well-off but she's got some independence about her. One of them sorts who thinks she can do it all herself. Don't like to admit it when she needs help. It's why she never went anywhere proper to get her house sorted."
"Just the sound of them over there pisses me off," Noggin says, passing him another can from a black bag at their feet.
Ranga cranes his neck to see if the chippy behind them is still closed. It is. "Him in there," he says, cocking a thumb towards the unlit takeaway window, "he's upped his fucking prices since them cunts took over The Swan."
A burst of laughter comes from a tall bamboo fence shielding the beer garden of a pub next door to the fish-and-chip shop. Ranga hates the pub since it reopened. The place was formerly boarded up for donkeys' years, since he was in his late teens at least, and then some posh cunt from the city bought it, did it up, and changed it into a fucking trendy bar. Now it is full of university students and upper-class wankers in suits. Scumbags like he and Noggin aren't welcome. Salt of the fucking earth cunts who grew up on these fucking streets, skinned their knees and climbed the trees, weren't fucking welcome in boozers their old 'uns practically fucking raised them in. It's not on. No fucking way, and it boils his fucking blood.

And Nogs is right, the sound of their voices is fucking grating. They are all pretentious fucking wankers with their no-accents from spending years away at university trying to lose their fucking roots, using long words and thinking they are better than the likes of him just because they've got money and fucking degrees. His old man had drunk in that pub, he had his first taste of beer there, and now it's a fucking shit shower.

"Some of the birds are alright though, eh, Rang?" Noggin says, nudging Ranga from his reverie with an elbow.

"Fuck 'em, I wouldn't touch them with yours," Ranga spits. He hates the nickname, short for 'orangutan' due to the colour of his hair; that and Noggin are the remnants of a gang life long since dead and gone.

A taxi pulls up outside the newly refurbed pub and spills a quartet of glamorous looking girls. *They can't even use the fucking bus, for fuck's sake.* He can't deny their desirability, but their Hollywood fakeness is out of place here. Two of them glance his way and he sees something pass between them before one mimes sticking her fingers down her throat then pretends to vomit.

"Fucking cunts!" Ranga shouts, his rage always rising dangerously quick to the surface like a deep-sea diver about to get the bends. He hurls his half-empty can at their feet and scowls at them as they flinch and jump back. The women look at him as if he is something they have trodden in and swiftly move past a pair of burly-looking bouncers and into the safety of the pub. Ranga thrusts his head towards the doormen. "Fucking take you two fucking apes as well!"

The pair laugh at his outburst and one speaks into a walkie-talkie. Cunts are probably permanently linked up to the police, like the security pricks in town. Ranga backs off and stands seething next to Noggin; seeing their stash bag blowing away empty adds to that anger. Loud cheers come from the secluded beer garden, maybe due to the arrival of the four girls, and he can picture them all drinking their expensive foreign piss-beers, celebrating some shit that means they will be getting an even bigger fucking wage packet, no doubt. He hates them. Some of the cunts are probably even local, growing up on the same fucking streets as him and acting high and mighty just because they have money and fucking qualifications. He digs his fingernails into his palms.

"Ranga, mate," Noggin says, with more than a hint of suspicion. "What the fuck you up to?"

Ranga picks up one of the black bin bags from the pavement outside the takeaway and holds it at arm's length as it drips putrid-smelling juices. Noggin's shock only encourages him. He launches the sack over the bamboo fence and hears a wonderful medley of shrieking and broken glass that reaches an ear-splitting crescendo as somebody lets out a deathly scream that seems endless. They both run like fuck.

"Haha, your fucking face when that bitch started bawling," Noggin says when he catches up with Ranga. "You were fucking shitting yourself, mate."

"The fuck I was!" Ranga pants, hands on knees, catching his breath.

"You fucking were." Noggin pats his friend on the back affectionately. "You were shitting it, man, ahaha."

Ranga snatches Noggin's wrist, twists his arm, and slams him face-first into a shop shutter. Noggin's nose squishes against the rusted metal; he barely has the chance to make a sound before Ranga growls in his ear. "You fucking calling me a fucking pussy?"

"No, no, Ranga, man," Noggin slurs through the side of

his squashed, bloodied mouth. Ranga grabs his hair and grinds his face into the filthy shutter, delighting in the sound of splintering bone on metal. "I am not a fucking pussy, you fucking cunt!" He shoves him one last time and then backs off, allowing Noggin to stumble away from the shop front, face like roadkill, hands thrashing uselessly like a de-stringed puppet, dripping blood and spitting tooth-chips.

Ranga grins at his handiwork. "I ain't a fucking pussy." His friend nods weakly.

"Right," Ranga says, and slides a wiry arm around his friend's shoulders. "Let's get you cleaned up and then you can buy us some more beer for being such a cunt."

Dream World

When Niamh sees the house, her breath is taken away. There is nothing spectacular about the bricks and mortar, but it seems to radiate affection. This house feels cherished. She can't help but smile as she crosses from the pavement to the front door. The exuberance spilling from the building makes her want to laugh and spin with childish glee. Philippa has chosen well; this is a happy, happy home.

The Way Old Friends Do

The excitement of her best mate coming over for the first time is depleted by the potential of Niamh putting a taint on the place before she has even been there a month-and-a-half. She is her oldest, closest friend and she loves her more than anything in the world but no matter how much Philippa tries, she can't make herself share Niamh's beliefs. She doesn't believe in spirits, or the ridiculous notion that buildings and objects can absorb the energy of previous owners and situations.

Philippa has made the place her own, got rid of the tobacco smell, and furnished the place throughout. It is *her* home now and she is determined that nothing is going to change the way she feels about it.

The doorbell rings and she whispers to the house, "If any ghosts could please fuck off right now, that would be great. Thanks."

She can see Niamh's colourful blur through the frosted glass in the door as she steps back and cranes her neck, looking up at the house. She has visions of the stereotypical extra-sensitive aunt in all haunted house movies who takes one foot inside her relative's home only to rush off in a flurry of palpitations and Hail Marys. *Please, Neem.* Philippa presses her forehead against the front door, steeling herself for her friend's first (and possibly only) visit to her new home.

"Phil!" Niamh's usual vibrancy is unexpected here and Philippa almost flinches when she flings her arms around her.

"Wow!" Philippa says, pulling her friend inside, revelling in her upbeat mood. "Look at you! New hair."

Niamh puts a hand to her bright purple, shoulder-length

hair. "This month's colour. To be honest, it'll probably stay this colour for a while."

Philippa yanks at a strand of her own dark blonde hair. "I can't remember the last time I went to the hairdressers."

"Let me do it for you." Niamh focuses on Philippa's hair as she follows her into the living-room.

They perch on the sofa and talk about girlie stuff for five minutes before Philippa offers to make a drink. Niamh hasn't mentioned the house yet, which is strange in itself. Isn't that the done thing when visiting a best friend's new place?

She is in the kitchen making coffee when it happens, when Niamh floats in like the ghosts she always speaks about, and broaches the subject. As ever, Niamh's habit of knowing exactly what is on Philippa's mind is uncannily accurate. Niamh stands to her side, her fingertips resting on the work surface, poised and grinning, reminding her of the CGI meerkats on those telly adverts.

"What?" Philippa can't stand her unnaturally happy face any longer. Niamh's default setting has been Grumpy Emo since they were in their teens. This is unsettling.

"You can't feel it, can you?" Niamh says, fixing Philippa with her rich brown eyes, "but it's definitely flowing through you. I can see it."

Oh, Christ, here we go. "Neem, what the fuck are you on about? You sound like a member of the bloody God squad right now, and frankly that would be more fucking scary than any of the ghost shit you've come out with."

Niamh laughs and spins full circle in the centre of the kitchen. "This place!"

"This place?"

Niamh nods and gazes around the ceiling and alcoves in a religious-like delirium. "It's so full of love. Whoever lived here before cherished this place and is so happy you're here."

It still freaks her out hearing about these types of presences and energies but at least it makes a change for it to be something positive for once.

Even as kids, Niamh insisted that she could hear and feel ghosts. She used to call them *leftovers* and said they were everywhere. Most of them were sad, or lost and confused. It used to spook Philippa out when she was little but Niamh reassured her that they wouldn't harm her because she was her friend, and that most of the leftovers only came back to visit, like a relative popping in to see a new baby. But Niamh always hated playing at Philippa's house. She did not like the old three-storey townhouse at all, something bad had happened there a long, long time ago and the black, shadowy repercussions still reverberated around its walls.

"Apparently some old lady lived here for years, it's been on the market pretty much since she died." Philippa hands Niamh a cup of coffee and they head back into the lounge. "Don't really know anything other than that."

"Doesn't matter," Niamh says, taking a seat. "There are so many times where there's some sort of sour, off-putting presence when you move into a new home. It's why I've always had to search for loads of places when I've moved. So many previous feelings and emotions remain that are negative and that can affect your mental and physical health, whether you are susceptible to them or not. But this place is awesome. It's like whoever or whatever remains here, I'm not necessarily talking dead people, is radiating positive energy at you like a bloody tsunami. You've struck gold, babe. You should be so happy here."

Philippa feels herself well up with her own intense feelings of pride and joy. Niamh's genuine contentment is infectious.

My Love, My Life

The feeling remains as Niamh leaves her friend in her
small pocket of paradise. The house is a tropical island,
overflowing with the scents and fauna of a thousand
wonderful memories. The presence, not the kind of
leftover that usually makes itself known, is welcoming
and loving, the remnants of someone, or maybe more
than one, who has lived a full and happy existence.
They've passed on, she's sure, and this is their mark on
reality, or rather, super-reality, something for only those
in tune with the colours, feelings and sounds of the
extraordinary. She's walking on air. Perry Como sings in
her head about the pavement always staying beneath his
feet and all at once *she* is several storeys high knowing she
has been to the house where someone wonderful lived
and where someone who is equally wonderful *lives*.

Tiger

The Staffie pup chews at one of Ranga's old trainers, the muscles beneath its tan-coloured pelt already forming thick and strong.

"She gonna be a right cheeky one, Ranga, man," Noggin says from the half-collapsed settee.

"Nah, I keep all my bitches in check," Ranga says, as the pup gnaws.

"Reckon I should get Tay to set me up with a dog, too?"

"If you can afford it. Get a boy. We can breed and split the profits."

Their friend Tay has a lucrative enterprise going on. He breeds a variety of different dogs, and a few days after taking the person's money and giving them their new puppy, one of his associates steals the dog back. This one is a dud, though, it's no good, it has a distinctive white splodge slap-bang in the centre of its forehead.

"That sounds like a good plan, man. Although I don't like the idea of a dog destroying the place."

Ranga grunts. "Your place already looks fucking destroyed."

"Yeah, but piss and shit and stuff."

"What, you mean aside from your own?"

"Haha, you know what I mean. You gotta train the fucking things, man." Noggin pulls a face as the mutt's teeth tear through the upper part of Ranga's shoe.

"Training them's a piece of piss." He leans forward and snatches the old trainer away from the dog and sticks one of his brand-new Nikes under the dog's nose. "You have to instil fear and teach them who's boss. Just like I have with you." The dog sniffs the new shoe and its wide pink tongue flicks across the toe before it opens its mouth ready to bite. Ranga strikes out sharp and hard with his other foot, catching the animal in the ribs and sending it rolling across the dirty carpet. He pounces on top of it, his hand around its throat, and moves within inches of its shaking face.

"BAD DOG!" Ranga growls between clenched teeth, and squeezes until the dog yelps. He sits back down on the settee and the dog creeps away, all the while keeping its eyes on its new owner. Ranga smiles, hands back the old trainer, and pats its head. "Good girl." The dog approaches the shoe with caution, waiting for further confirmation or punishment. "Good girl," Ranga repeats, and the dog begins to worry at the shoe again, although not with the same enthusiasm this time. "See? It's all about fucking control. Don't matter how big the fucking dog is or nothing. It's all up here." He taps two fingers to his temple. "Oh, by the way, she's pissed on your floor."

Suzy-Hang-Around

Philippa has been on a high since Niamh's visit, she isn't sure whether it is something to do with her friend's unusual exuberance about her new home or a general good feeling. The love she feels for the place is incredible, everything is perfect.

She used to think that living alone would be a frightening experience for someone who had never been truly on their own before. Although as a child and adolescent she was never really popular, and had only ever really had Niamh and her parents, so she had imagined that this would be scary, but it isn't.

Since learning to love herself rather than hating the fat, pathetic whale she used to be, she has come to relish her solitude. Friends from the yoga classes and gym that she attends after her day at the office try to invite themselves on her early-morning runs, marvelling at her capacity to do all that before *and* after work. She meets their pleas with polite refusals; she will happily give them pointers, but for her, running is a solitary experience. It isn't only exercise but a form of meditation, an exhilarating experience that makes her feel alive like nothing else she has ever tried. So, it shouldn't come as such a surprise to find that living on her own feels akin to this, but it does. Every morning is a spiritual reawakening: she springs from the bed like an actor from a ludicrously cheesy commercial and bounces around the place, her house, getting ready for her run and preparing for work. Everything is set to a schedule that she sticks to come rain or shine, but this morning, her first day back at work after the move, she takes an alternate running route due to a car crash and she is going to be late.

There's an extra vibration to her heart after her run: she remembers she's supposed to be meeting Ryan later for that drink.

Everything is a rush.

Her running clothes are peeled off and discarded where they fall as she speeds towards the shower. One pro for living alone. She flicks the kettle on and grabs a banana as she runs through the kitchen in just her knickers.

Determined not to be late, Philippa quickly showers the sweat from her body, dries herself within two minutes, and runs back into the kitchen wrapped in two towels, half a banana resting between her lips like a fat cigar. She spoons coffee into her travel mug and yanks out a plastic caddy and adds sugar, her only vice, into the thermos before adding boiling water. The end of her banana breaks off and her hand jerks out to catch it before it hits the work surface. She is about to congratulate herself on her lightning reflexes when she sees the sugar caddy teeter, fall, and explode across the linoleum. "Fuck!" She'd barely even touched the damn thing.

The floor around her bare feet is dusted white. There is no way she is going to have time to clear that and get ready for the bus.

Another perk of living on her own: *leave the tidying until later.*

She hooks the travel mug with two fingers and turns to leave the kitchen to get dressed when she feels something shift in the air behind her. Goose pimples prickle the bare skin on her shoulders and she has the sudden urge to cover up. She laughs incredulously at her own out-of-character jumpiness, and to convince herself she is being stupid, spins around just in time and the kitchen is filled with fairy dust, at least that's what it looks like, fairy dust twinkling in the sunlight. A millisecond is all she gets to see of this wonder as the granules of sugar fall to the floor with a hiss.

The rush of getting dressed and to the bus stop is a blur. Philippa fights against what she saw, refuses to believe it. Grains of sugar floating in her kitchen. For a split second she did see it, that was the problem, the minuscule granules suspended in the air. Then they scattered across the lino.

Buildings and shops flash past the bus window but Philippa pays no attention to anything other than trying to solve this strange phenomenon. Talking to Niamh would only get the obvious answer: *It's the leftovers trying to communicate with you.*
She wishes she had a friend in physics as opposed to psychics. Some of the boys she knows from college studied something in the sciences but she could imagine their faces were she to broach the subject of floating sugar.
An internet search bears absolutely no fruit at all — unless she wants to know about fermentation.

By the time she gets to work, the scene is forced into the cluttered attic of her mind. It's up there in a dark corner in the box with the other unexplained mysteries of her life, like the valentine's day card from J when she was fourteen and the as-yet undiscovered dimension where pen lids, solitary socks, and scissors go.

Work is a trawl. Each time she looks at the clock, she thinks it's stopped.
Katherine comes in to say hello, she's still on sick leave and seeing the way she is knocks Philippa's mood off kilter for the rest of the day. Katherine's hair hides the patch and gauze over her right eye, and the scars where the glass splintered across her cheeks are nothing in comparison. She says she's alright but it's obvious she's anything but. She says the doctors are hopeful that some of the vision will return and the scarring will be minimal, but for someone like Katherine, looks mean everything. She wears her depression like an actual garment, a heavy, lead-lined fur cloak. Philippa can all but see it about her shoulders, but still, she insists she's fine. Katherine goes, and in her wake, leaves Philippa a vivid re-enactment of that afternoon in the beer garden of The Swan.

Laughter, drinks, everything is chilled and happy. Chris, Dave and Martin are there already, always the first to arrive and the last to leave.
Jeremy is a no-show as per usual, it is either work or women issues with him; this time it's work. Philippa is comfortable with the boys, even more so when she has Niamh by her side and is grateful that everyone gets on, especially with Niamh. A lot of people are iffy with Niamh to begin with. Philippa is used to the weirdo but some people take a while to warm to her.

Katherine and her trio of TOWIE clones are the last to arrive, they are glammed up to the nines and smell like a perfumery; they're probably going somewhere else later. Greetings and introductions to Zina, Erica and Francesca are made, drinks are fetched, and Niamh goes back to whatever heated debate she is having with Martin. Philippa thinks there's an underlying sexual chemistry between the two, despite their philosophical differences, and if only Martin would overlook Niamh's past, they would make an awesome couple.

Everything's great, meeting new people is alright, really, but out of Katherine's trio it's Zina who steals the show. She's an Indian princess studying to be a doctor and Philippa thinks she's beautiful. It's good to get to know her and she's hilarious as she tells them about their run-in with a couple of chavs outside the pub.

Then someone throws a spanner in the works and it comes in the form of a black bin bag.

Something fleetingly blocks out the sunlight; Chris cries out and pushes his chair back as a foul-dripping asteroid crashes right in the centre of the table, sending glass and garbage over everyone. Then Katherine is screaming, her hands are on her face, and there's blood running between her fingers.

Katherine isn't alright and she's worried her friend will never come back from something like that.

Philippa pushes away the horrific scene of blood and burst bin bags in time to knock off, stores it amongst remembered footage from horror films and her own real-life encounters.

She catches the bus amongst tired commuters and mentally reminds herself to get off one stop early by The Towers to meet Ryan.

Keep an Eye on Dan

Ranga's already been in there an hour. *A bit of Dutch courage whilst I'm here and got the money.* He's managed to stretch his latest government handout further than usual, the cash from stripping the house has helped with that. It makes a change to actually be doing something for a living and it's good to be in control. It isn't all above board, cash in hand, but since when has that changed anything? Noggin's a lazy fucker to work with, but Ranga makes sure to only pay him what he's worth. *Lazy cunt.* He thinks about the bird with the house, Philippa. She's fit as fuck, got a decent education by the sounds of it, but ain't got as many brains as she thinks she has. Just because you've got the academic results on paper doesn't mean you've got what it takes to get through real life. She's a good few years younger, too, birds like an older bloke.

He checks himself out in a mirror behind the bar as he orders another bottle. *Looking good.* The young piece behind the counter has already been giving him the eye, *dirty little nympho.* She doesn't look old enough to work behind a bar, can't be long out of school. She's a looker, though: mixed race, big eyes, big lips. Ranga smirks and waggles his empty lager bottle. *Big tits and big arse, too. Maybe if things don't go to plan tonight, I'll come back and get this one's number.*

*

Ryan's scrubbed up well but Philippa can't help but miss the sight of him in his paint-flecked scruffs. She waves at him and rushes to the bar before he can act all chivalrous and try to buy her a drink.

"Alright, stranger, long time no see," the barmaid says, and it takes Philippa far too long to put a name to the familiar face. It's her schoolmate Freya Williams' little sister. Keisha? Keida? Kayla? She curses her memory but smiles in recognition. "Hiya, how long you been working here?"

"Couple of months," K says, and leans across the bar.

"What are you doing in here?"

"Got a date, haven't I?"

Keisha, it's definitely Keisha. Philippa thanks God for the landlord and their insistence on staff wearing name badges. Keisha's big hazel eyes flicker back and forth between her and Ryan. "The ginger, has a Japanese tattoo on his forearm, thinks he's a hard man?"

Philippa nods. "I'm not prejudiced."

"Yeah, me neither. Each to their own, innit? Not my type, bit scrawny and too old..."

"Well, thank you for your opinion..."

"...Too male and all," she whispers, seemingly, unsure and leans on the bar.

"Oh!" Philippa didn't see that one coming, but the last time she saw her, Keisha was fourteen, smoking fags up by the playing fields with a couple of rough-looking lads. "Yeah, blokes are crap." Keisha sniggers and seems to remember she's supposed to be working. "What can I get you?"

Philippa orders a gin and lemonade and asks after Freya, Keisha's older sister.

"Six months pregnant! Daft cow."

Philippa is shocked. Shocked by how she's let another schoolmate slip out of her web. All these mental reminders that she'll contact them soon repeatedly put on snooze until eventually she forgets and they have the audacity to carry on with their own lives without letting her know. She is sure she has Freya's number and adds yet another mental reminder to the ever-increasing list. She walks towards Ryan with thoughts of her schoolmate and potential baby showers and has forgotten all about her by the time she gets to the table.

Lovelight

That went well, Philippa thinks as she walks back home. Ryan was a gentleman, offered to walk with her, but she politely refused as she knew what such things could lead to and she wasn't ready for that - yet. Ryan was just as nice as he had been when her dad was around, didn't try to sleaze all over her or anything, which is what she had expected. She kept her promise to herself that she would only stop for two drinks, nothing too serious for a first date, this was really only an ice-breaker to see if he had potential. He hinted at a rough upbringing but never went into any morbid details and was happy when she said that she wasn't proud of her younger years either. She remembers she has to message Freya and congratulate her on her pregnancy, which in turn makes her consider another note to Katherine to ask her how she's really feeling. Sometimes it's easier for people to tell the truth via a keypad. All this and she's decided to go for a second date with Ryan by the time she reaches the low brick wall of her front garden.

The house welcomes her like a protective parent as she steps across the threshold leaving her troubles outside in the dark. It's warm, pleasant, and smells amazing, a mixture of flora and happy memories.
She can't help but smile as she switches on a light and hangs up her jacket.
This is my house.

She can't wait to have everyone around; the place is almost ready, just one or two more items of furniture and maybe some flowers. Philippa doesn't know where that thought came from, as she's never really been bothered about such things before, but then again, she's never had her own place before. She rests on the settee and wonders whether the previous tenant's tastes have somehow rubbed off on her, but realises that's the kind of nonsense Niamh would talk about.

She remembers to sweep up the fallen sugar crystals and glass from the kitchen lino before running her bath.

Mamma Mia

There's a lump on the inside of her left thigh and it fucking hurts. She doesn't know whether it's the pain of the bite that's woken her, or the throbbing of the venom afterwards. *I've been bitten.* Upon this realisation, Philippa leaps from her bed and strips off the duvet in one swift motion, expecting to see striped evil crawling across her sheets. There's nothing she can see in the bed. She carefully stands in the light of the window and inspects her wound. Raised and red with a deep pinprick in the centre. It feels like a wasp sting, looks like one too, and there's nothing remaining where it pricked her. "Fucking bastard thing."

She's not going to put anything on it if she doesn't know exactly what caused it. A childhood memory resurfaces of her mother putting a spray for wasp stings on her bee stings when she was a child and her arms swelling up twice their size.

Philippa stomps through the bungalow littering the rooms with a variety of different curse words on her way to the bathroom. At the back of he remind the estate agent's words about the wasp nest in the attic worry at her but she tells herself she's being irrational. Cold water eases the pain, but not her bad mood.

There's an answerphone notification on her mobile - work - and she feels like it's going to be one of those days where she'll wish she'd stayed in bed. She's meant to be going to the park with Ryan; he wants her to meet his dog, *bless him*, but seeing the number of her office tells her that's probably out of the window now. More inventive profanity puffs from her mouth as she presses and swipes and calls her boss, Hannah, who answers immediately.

"Hi, Hannah, it's me. You rang?" She says, trying hard not to sound pissed off.

"Hi, Pip, did you not listen to the message?" Hannah says hurriedly. There's a lot of noise in the background, her colleagues dealing with clients at the call centre.

"No..."

"It's okay, I just asked if you'd call back about eleven when I'm on my break, but it's okay."

Philippa breathes a slight sigh of relief; by the sounds of it, her day's plans don't have to be cancelled. "What's up?" Hannah is silent for a long time, it's only the background humdrum that tells her the line is still connected. "I don't know how to tell you this. It's easier with the others who are in today, you know, telling them face to face."

Oh, shit. Philippa instantly thinks she's going to lose her job. She looks around at her beautiful house and her heart leaps into her throat at the thought of having to give it up and move back in with her parents.

"It's okay, nothing to worry about," Hannah says, "it's just that we got some really bad news this morning."

"What?"

"I don't know how to say this so I'm just going to come out with it. Katherine took her own life last night. An overdose."

Philippa slaps her hand over her mouth to muffle the moan that escapes.

"Her mum said she went downhill when the doctors couldn't save the sight in her eye, and the scarring. You know what she was like."

Philippa presses her thumb and forefinger against her own eyes as though doing so will erase the images of her friend's face, of that bursting black bag coming over the beer garden fence.

"Look, Pip, it's really busy here, I've got to go. I'll call you later, okay?"

"Okay, Hannah, thanks for telling me. Oh, my god!" Philippa mumbles, the last part comes out as a cry, along with her tears, and she hangs up before her boss can hear her.

Lovers (Live a Little Longer)

She rings Ryan to cancel after hearing the news about Katherine but he persuades her to come, tells her he's really looking forward to it, that coming out will make her feel better, and adds a layer of guilt by saying Layla, his dog, is looking forward to it too.

The day outside is as lifeless as her friend: dull, grey, with not a speck of warmth.

Katherine is all she can think about as she walks towards the park, the air dampening the skin on cheeks that haven't stayed dry since her boss's phone call. Philippa wonders whether Katherine went peacefully, like falling into a deep, comfortable sleep, but has horrific images of her lying across soiled sheets with green, crusted foam around her lips and matte, sightless eyes. She tries to push her from her mind but Katherine is everywhere she looks, even in the park.

She takes a side entrance, a shortcut to meet Ryan at the main one, and Katherine is there in the green leaves on the trees, the same shade as her eyes, and she's there in the dog litter bin which overflows with black plastic parcels, miniature replicas of the bag of shit that indirectly killed her. She spots Ryan's lanky figure by the elaborate arches, even the black of his tracksuit against the red Victorian brickwork reminds her of death and blood.

A brown-and-white dog stands statue-still at his feet; she wants to turn back, go, fly away home where it's safe and sound. Breath comes in short, intermittent fever-bursts, it's a panic attack but she doesn't know it. What she does know is that being at home, in her house, swaddled by blankets, will make her safe.

She turns to go and he sees her, she hears her name called across the expanse. Unfamiliar anger sparks up somewhere in her chest and overwhelms the rising panic. Anger at this fucking chav for making her come out when she really didn't want to. She forces herself to continue walking, one step at a time, swallows the anger along with the panic, and wonders if Katherine's pills were just as hard to stomach.

A smile comes as she sees the dog; it's not on a lead and is grinning stupidly like all good dogs do; eye contact with Ryan will bring tears and she doesn't want to share those with him yet.

As man and dog get closer, she hears him say, "Go and say hello." The dog bounds forward excitedly, tongue flapping; she has a little white dot on her forehead, like a bindi. Philippa crouches and the dog rushes at her but stays on four feet, she's been trained not to jump. Philippa loses herself and wraps her arms around the animal and lets it cover her with licks and sniffs, excited as it is by the new smells and places. It's been too long since she's felt the unconditional, innocent, love of an animal. She hasn't had a dog since her parents' Labrador died when she was fourteen.

"Jesus," Ryan says, "dog gets a better greeting than I do." Philippa squints up, her face half-buried in the dog's scruff, tears now covered in a light sprinkling of short brown-and-white fur. "I think it's love at first sight."

"For you or Layla?"

Philippa stands but Layla is glued to her hip. She glances down at the beautiful creature's golden eyes. "I think the feeling is mutual."

"Thank god for that. It's always scary introducing your new bird to your kid," Ryan says with a sheepish grin, and is pleased when Philippa laughs at his joke.

He's so happy that he has to repeat the line one more time. However, her second laugh is one hundred percent fake.

They take a walk by the lake, where Ryan tells her that he and Noggin have another decorating job lined up the following week. Layla potters ahead, sniffing at every post to read previous dogs' scents.

She tells him about Katherine, and the incident in the beer garden which started her decline, and she's touched by the emotion Ryan shows on his face. For a moment, he's lost for words, and she decides to hold his hand, happy that there's a more sensitive side to him, that he isn't as bolshy as she thought he was.

They have a coffee in the park café.

Layla barks at the ducks but as soon as Ryan growls her name she's at his side, tail tucked beneath her hind legs, rump a-quiver.

Philippa tells him to leave Layla be, *she's a fucking dog, for Christ's sake, and she's no chance in hell of catching one of the feathery bastards*, and after giving Philippa a strange look, he lets Layla run amok amongst a flock of pecking ducks. It pleases Philippa to see the dog running around excitedly; not once does she try to attack any of the birds, she just runs with them, idiot grin, tongue flapping, undiluted happiness. *Leave her be, let her be.* Layla comes straight to Philippa when she calls her name, the same signs of joyous affection bestowed, mutually, and Ryan is shocked and disgruntled. "Are you the fucking dog whisperer, or something?"

Philippa laughs, as happy as the dog, and presses her lips against Ryan's, surprising him, surprising herself. Layla surprises them both by jumping up, trying to get in between them. Ryan lashes out, striking the dog in the chest and knocking her to the floor. She lands awkwardly but rights herself.

"What the fuck was that?" Philippa demands, hugging the dog.

Ryan is crestfallen, ashamed. "Err...she knows not to jump up. I've got a thing about dogs getting in my face." The way he spits words sounds like he's making up an excuse on the spot.

Philippa feels like she has no choice other than to believe him; it's his dog, after all. "Okay, well, don't push her like that. She responds well enough to verbal commands, doesn't she?"

"Yeah, yeah." He pats the dog's head half-heartedly. "She's just a bit reckless. Fearless," he says. He rolls up his sleeve and shows her a tattooed symbol on his forearm. "Like me."

"Maybe she's jealous that someone's muscling in on her man?" Philippa says with a smirk, thinking about the barmaid's words about him being a hard man. She leans against him and looks down at the dog. "Are you a jealous baby girl, Layla? Does you want daddy all to yourself?"

The dog growls low in its throat as the couple hug, and Philippa laughs. "Oh, you got yourself a jealous woman right there, Ryan."

"Yeah, well, she can piss off!" he says, and quickly adds fake laughter in an attempt to transform a serious statement into one of humour.

"She's just got to get used to it, that's all," Philippa says, and leans in for another kiss. Layla's low growl is thunder on the horizon.

"No, Layla," Philippa scolds, and Layla ceases growling, pines, and lies down at their feet.

"Definitely a dog whisperer," Ryan says, and the kisses continue.

The romantic feeling remains for the rest of their time in the park, surrounding them like a bubble, making colours brighter and everything nicer.

It even accompanies them as Ryan and Layla walk her back to the house, and it takes all the willpower Philippa can muster not to let the man and the adorable dog across the threshold.

She knows exactly what it would lead to, and she doesn't want their first time to be due to the flurry of emotions caused by her friend's suicide.

Ryan and Layla leave her at the front door, and both walk off mournfully with their tails between their legs.

Philippa lets herself in and goes straight to bed to cry. To cry because of Katherine, and to cry because of the company she's had to refuse in case she couldn't trust herself to let it become more. She crawls into bed and wishes Ryan had left Layla with her.

Philippa has been crying in her sleep; her cheeks are wet, but soft, warm fingertips brush the tears away as a gentle hand strokes her head. She is at home, and a child. Her mum always does this when she has nightmares, never wakes her for fear of increasing the fright, just comforts her like all good mothers should. Philippa nestles into the softness, letting her mother's caress soothe her almost back to sleep, when she remembers Katherine, and remembers that she isn't a child anymore. She's up with a start and the room is sunny and warm and smells of citrus and flowers and the air beside the bed shifts as something invisible, sensed rather than seen, drifts away like a dream.

The floral odour dissipates and Philippa sits startled on the edge of the bed.

Me and Bobby and Bobby's Brother

The fucking barmaid is giving me the eye again. He's only come in the pub because it was on the way back from Philippa's and they let you bring your dog in. She has a right cheeky grin on her and comes over to chat to him when she's not serving the half dozen old gits dotted around the joint. "What's your dog's name?" she asks, wiping the tabletop, even though it doesn't need wiping. "Layla," Ranga says with a grin, and peers down her cleavage as she leans over the table.

"Aw, 'sa nice name." She hasn't asked, but crouches down and fusses the dog. Layla loves the attention; Ranga loves the way the barmaid's jeans cling to her buttocks. "So, what's your name?" he asks as he drains his bottle. "Keisha."

"What's a nice girl like you doing working here?" That's how it starts, casual banter which mutates into flirting, and before either of them knows it, they're both back at Ranga's dingy flat. Layla is immediately shut in a kitchen that's caked in dog shit and puddles of urine. Ranga briefly wonders what Keisha's game is when she readily accepts his invite back to his place but when she asks him if he's carrying anything, or got anything back at his, he figures it out.

"Yeah, course I have." He pauses. "Well, depends what you're after, don't it? It'll cost you, though, I don't give freebies."

She thrusts herself towards him, chest-first, on his semi-collapsed settee. Her tongue is in his mouth within seconds and she fumbles with his tracksuit bottoms; she tastes of cigarettes and Tia Maria.

Ranga has her naked, on all fours, and mounted before he even knows what it is she's really after — and he doesn't really care. Layla whines from her kitchen prison and scratches at the conjoining door as she hears rapid grunting and the smacking of flesh upon flesh. Afterwards, Keisha seems a bit pissed off that all Ranga has to offer is a couple of joints. He calls her an ungrateful cunt and tells her to get the fuck out.

Gonna Sing You My Love Song

"Hey, the place is looking great," Niamh says, dropping her bag and settling onto the settee. Her hair is green this month and she's had it cut into a pixie bob with long, pointy side bits. Philippa is jealous that her friend seems to reinvent herself on a monthly basis and always gets it fresh and right.

Niamh doesn't look for the usual things that most people notice when visiting their friends: new furniture, ornaments, and such. Instead, she seems to scrutinise the very air, the ambiance of the room, the invisible things every day folk can't see. Her sensitivity gives her an air of mystique, sometimes she appears dazed. Philippa barely notices this now, though, as she's used to her friend and her 'leftovers.'

"How you holding up after the news about Katherine?" Niamh says sympathetically.

"I'm coming to terms with it. It's just so tragic."

Niamh nods. "Is that why you wanted me to come around? To ask about her?"

Philippa is confused by Niamh's questioning, slow when it comes to realising what she's hinting at. Her perplexity is obvious.

"I haven't heard or seen anything," Niamh says quietly, uncomfortably, in the knowledge that Philippa has never truly believed in her abilities.

"Oh," Philippa starts, "oh, no. No. I wasn't going to ask about that. Umm..." She feels her face flush.

"Is this something to do with your new man?"

"No, no. Jeez, woman, would you let me talk? I mean, this is hard for me."

"What is?"

Philippa looks around the room and laughs. "Admitting that I might be one step closer to believing in you and your leftovers."

Niamh physically jolts, her hands clasp at her small chest and grab the material there and she lets out an excited noise that's more bark than laugh. "What's happened?"

Philippa tells her about the weird episode with the sugar and the more recent incident in the bedroom.

"It's the old lady."

Philippa smiles and is surprised to find herself nodding. "I... I can't believe I'm going to say this but, yes, yes, I think so."

Niamh explodes with excitement, grabs her hands and hugs her. "I told you this place was good."

"Yeah. Do you think she is here for a reason?"

"Maybe. Maybe not. I think they're just free to do whatever the hell they like without the restrictions of earthly bodies. Despite me being in tune with them I don't really know that much. I think they like to watch, to visit, to remember."

"The stuff you used to tell me when we were kids scared the shit out of me."

"Sorry," Niamh says with a snigger. "I didn't mean to."

"I thought you were proper cray-cray, but my parents said most kids have overactive imaginations, especially when it comes to scary things."

"Yeah, but you hear lots of stories about babies and toddlers and how they tell of friendly visitors they've had in their bedrooms at night that no one else has ever seen and when asked to describe them, they give accurate descriptions of relatives dead long before they were born."

"I just assumed they'd seen photos or something."

"Yeah. Maybe some, but others do see things the majority of people can't."

It's been a long, long time since Philippa has discussed Niamh and her gift and she has a thousand questions. "I remember you saying that your grandparents used to come and stand at the end of your bed at night. That scared the hell out of me."

Niamh smiles sadly. "They don't come so often when you're grown up. I think when they knew I could see them and we could communicate, it gave them the energy to come back again and again. I don't really know how it works, and to tell you the truth, I don't think those who have passed on do either, really."

"Do you see them, the leftovers, ghosts all over the place?"

"No, they're quite rare, to be honest. I think most move on somewhere else but some linger for whatever reason. I don't *see* anything very often, that's only happened a few times, mostly it's a presence, a pressure, a twinkling in the air that no one else seems to notice.

"Sometimes it's smells, or on rare occasions, noises and sensations.

"It's like the feeling that someone is watching you, or just nosing over your shoulder, but when you turn to look there's no one there."

"Wow!" Philippa plants her face in her hands and finds herself in tears.

Niamh laughs. "You daft bint, why you getting all emotional?"

"It's beautiful, if it's true, to know that some part of us, of Katherine, even if it's just elemental, goes on."

Niamh hugs her and Philippa sees tears in her eyes too.

"You sure you're not frightened? I can try to communicate if you are."

"Oh, God, no." Philippa looks towards the light fittings in embarrassment as though the previous tenant is floating up there, eavesdropping. "She makes me feel safe. The house feels safe and loved. The estate agent said she had no family, so maybe she wants someone to look after."
"I'm just hoping she can tolerate me for the evening after I've had half a bottle of this." Niamh pulls a pink bottle from her bag, it's decadent and is designed to look antiquated, a novel flavour gin.
Philippa laughs. "Hey, I'm sure she'd love a girls' night in."

Dancing Queen

There's a heady atmosphere in the living room that makes her think of fields and summer festivals. They've taken their shoes off and they're dancing on the new plush carpet in bare feet. Philippa's stuck a nineties' playlist on, tracks from when they were kids, and the songs remind them of happy times. Niamh has made her dress up even though they aren't leaving the house and it feels great. The room buzzes with lavender, violets, and something citric, it's exhilarating, as though their uplifted mood is charging the air itself. Cut grass, sticky sweets, chocolate, candy floss, vinegar, chips, and sea air. Happy smells, a welcome invasion.

Niamh screams unnaturally high when a song comes on that she's not heard for years and she spins on the spot, just like they used to do when they were children.

After a fashion they fall in a heap on the sofa where they refill their glasses with pink gin and lemonade.

"Do you think Nelly's having a good time?" Niamh rests her head against Philippa's.

Philippa answers with a laugh. "Who the fuck's Nelly?"

"Oh, I've decided that's what we're calling your ghost, unless she makes herself known and tells me otherwise."

Philippa lets out a series of drunken cackles and calls out, "Nelly? Nelly? You like our music?" She puts her phone on the table and opens up her music app. "If you have any requests, knock yourself out." She can barely contain her laughter.

Philippa slumps back onto the settee and the pair of them discover they are both at that infectious level of drunkenness where virtually anything can be funny. Niamh flicking her fingernail against her glass making a *ping* noise almost causes Philippa's bladder to burst. The current track finishes and an ABBA song starts, and they both look at one another in shock for a second before the laughter returns. As Niamh drags her off the sofa to dance to 'Dancing Queen,' Philippa wonders what the song is doing on a nineties' playlist.

The song reminds Philippa of when she was really little, when Granny Frances was still alive, and, for some reason, Christmas. Granny Frances with her short-cropped hair and corduroy trousers, and jumpers that she knitted herself. Granny Frances, who was her mother's mother, but as there was never a man mentioned in the scenario, it was as if her mum had been immaculately conceived. Granny Frances and her mum had been ABBA fans, and this song always brings her to mind, sat in the corner, ever-knitting, getting older and older until she just wasn't there anymore.

The lyrics are ingrained; Philippa sings along without even realising she's doing it, and when the song fades and 'Thank You For the Music' comes on, she breaks into it without hesitation.

It's Niamh who stops her, but it's indirectly, her face wide open with fantastical wonder as she looks at Philippa's phone.

"Phil, this isn't the nineties' playlist. Did you change it? Tell me you did!" Niamh's fingers hover above the phone screen, not touching. "Come here, give me your hand."

"What the fuck, Neem?" Philippa says giddily, but gives her friend her hand. The air above them is several degrees cooler than the rest of the room but it's not a draught, it tingles and tickles like the lightest of snow flurries. Cogs whir in Philippa's alcohol-addled mind and she sees that a glitch on her music app has switched from the playlist to the best of ABBA. At least that's what the rational side of her mind tells her. *A glitch.* The cold, not unpleasant, snowflake feeling vanishes and there's a knock at the front door that scares the shit out of them both.

Don't Shut Me Down

Three sheets to the wind. Where the fuck does that expression come from? Philippa wonders as she flies from the surreal experience in the lounge to answer the front door. It was something her mum and Granny Frances used to say when they were describing a drunk. It was either that or 'half-cut.' She's more than half-cut; she balances herself on the hallway walls and hopes whoever it is has fucked off by the time she reaches the door.

"Hang on," Philippa slurs at the dark red wood as she unfastens bolts and chains. She opens the door, cursing her drunken self in that brief moment for not having looked through the spyhole. It could be anyone.

"Oh." She's relieved but confused to see Ryan and Layla standing out in just the light from the house. Layla leaps up at her before Ryan can tell her not to.

"I was passing this way," he says, and she notices him eyeing up the hallway behind her. "Just thought we'd come and say hello on the way home, like."

She doesn't let him in. "Ryan, mate, it's like ten o'clock. I thought you were out with your mates tonight?"

He shifts uncomfortably on his feet. "Yeah, I was, but we got that job to start in the morning so we called it an early one."

Philippa smiles and gives him a quick hug and a kiss.

"Well, go and get some sleep and take this beautiful lady with you."

His crestfallen expression flips to mild annoyance at her subtle refusal. "You got company?" He tries to look past her, as though if he cranes his neck an extra few centimetres he'll reveal all the secrets of the covenant.

"Just my friend, Niamh, that's all. We're having a girls'
night in." Philippa has strong feelings towards this man
but at the moment he is not taking the hint. She wants
him to fuck off home to bed and longs to be able to tell
him that without the danger of repercussion. Another
fake smile rests on a pair of lips that crave more gin.
"Look, babe, come around tomorrow night, and we'll
have a drink and stuff."

Ryan stares at her and for a few seconds he's a different
man: cold, malevolent, but then he grins. "Sounds good."
He pushes past her. "Gotta use your toilet first, though.
I'm gasping, sorry."

Philippa is gobsmacked. She hears him pass through the
lounge, hears him say hello to Niamh on his way towards
the bathroom at the back. From the doormat, Layla looks
up at her affectionately.

"Who's that?" Niamh asks, appearing beside her and
melting on sight of the dog.

"Oh, that's Ryan, and this is Layla," Philippa says,
shocked by his intrusion but trying her best to tell herself
it's no big deal.

"Hello, Layla." Niamh crouches beside the dog for a fuss,
the glance she gives Philippa saying more than words.

"It's okay, he's not stopping," Philippa mutters.

"No, don't go getting your knickers in a twist, love. Just
passing and needed to use the toilet." Ryan surprises
them both, and Philippa catches him looking at Niamh's
exposed thighs as she crouches besides his dog.

"That was quick," Philippa says, not quite managing to
keep the sarcasm from her voice. *Quickest piss in history.*
Extra-sensitive, Niamh senses the building tension and
excuses herself.

"I ain't checking up on you," Ryan says defensively.
That's exactly what you're doing. "I never said you were."

"You don't bloody have to," he says, and he's getting angrier.

"Look, I'll take your word for it, okay?"

"To be honest with you, Layla got excited when we were walking past."

Philippa weakens a little at the mention of the dog but doesn't know whether it's true or emotional blackmail. "Really?"

"Yeah," Ryan says, calming down. Smiling, he scratches behind one of Layla's ears. "She, well, *we,* we like you, don't we?"

"The feeling's mutual, you know?" She looks at Layla when she says this, maybe she should give him the benefit of the doubt. Guilt begins to surface that she's sending them both away but she forces herself to think of Niamh. Niamh likes to be forewarned before meeting anyone new, especially men. She chews her lip and tries to find the right words to make them both leave. "Look, I mean it, about tomorrow —"

Niamh crashes past them, white as a sheet, bag in hand.

"I'm sorry, Pip." Her words are barely decipherable.

Philippa reaches for her friend, feels the light brush of her dress against her fingertips as she slips by.

"I have to go. I'm sorry." Niamh blurts the words out as fast as she can without turning back.

Niamh's sudden departure floors Philippa, literally: she's on her arse in the doorway with Ryan and the dog standing over her, both looking as stupid as one other. She's never done anything like this before, in all the years they've been friends.

"Neem?" Philippa calls quietly into the night, but her friend has gone.

"So, you gonna let us in now?" Ryan doesn't wait for an answer and enters her paradise once more, without her consent.

Gimme! Gimme! Gimme! (A Man After Midnight)

She's nervous, that's her problem. Ranga knows what women like Philippa are like. They think they're all independent because they've got their own digs and stuff but deep down they just need a bloke who will take the bull by the horns. He sits beside her on her settee as her anger slowly subsides and she starts rabbiting on about her weirdo mate who fucked off. She's kneading Layla's scruff like dough, and they both seem to find it therapeutic. The dog's snoring, head on her lap, and Philippa has calmed down.

Ranga offers meaningless sentiments as Philippa's annoyance is completely overtaken by the sudden disappearance of her friend. She repeatedly rings Niamh's phone number and it's obvious she is rejecting the call. Ranga knows how he should play this.

"I'm sorry I made your mate feel like she had to go." The expression on Philippa's face tells him that's exactly what she's thinking too, but he wonders if she's brave enough to admit it. "You didn't make her go, but she does usually like to be forewarned before meeting new people."

"I'm sorry, if I had known you had company..."

Philippa sighs and puts down her phone. "Oh well, it's done now. It's not like her to leave like that. I hope everything is okay."

"Look, I'm sure she'll message you or whatever."

Philippa nods and leans back into the sofa.

"Come on, let's have a drink and chill for a bit, yeah?
She'll probably call you when she gets home and I don't
want to leave you whilst you're upset." Ranga pretends
not to notice her shake her head and pours the rest of the
pink gin into the pair of glasses on the table. He sees her
lips move and cuts in first, handing her the glass. "There
you go, get it down you. Doctor's orders."
The alcohol has the desired effect on Philippa. She chills
the fuck out about her airy-fairy friend and leans into him
for idle chatter. He thinks about her mate for a few
seconds and wonders whether she is going to be a
problem. She is a well hot problem, like Tinkerbell with
tits, even though she did seem like a snooty bitch for
fucking off without so much as a hello. Philippa's talking
about her, saying she's known her almost all her life and
blah blah blah, he's not really listening and her speech is
slurred and getting quieter and quieter and he looks at
her and her chin is bobbing towards her chest, her eyelids
virtually closed.
Ranga carefully takes her glass off her. "Come on, let's get
you to bed."

Andante, Andante

Philippa wakes up and wonders how she got into bed.
Considering how Ryan persuaded his way into the house
the night before, she's surprised he's not in bed beside
her, surprised she's still fully clothed. Then guilt bubbles
up for thinking the worst of him, for not having faith in
her judgement of character. She's not happy that she'd let
herself get so bloody drunk, but that only happened
because she was expecting a night in with Niamh. She's
angry that she let that situation happen and she's angry
with Ryan that he didn't go when she told him to, but
smothering all that is her ongoing concern for Niamh. She
forces herself from the bed, ignoring the dull throb in her
head, and searches for her phone. It's nowhere to be seen.
The fleeting annoyance of waking up with a low phone
battery pesters her; she always charges it at night, has her
routines. Her phone's on the coffee table in the living
room, Ryan's asleep on the sofa, Layla is sprawled out on
the floor, and the room reeks of tobacco. Fury about his
smoking in her house threatens to boil over but she
doesn't know how the dog will react to a sudden
outburst. She grabs her phone and plugs it in to charge
and hears Layla yawn, stretch, and the flapping of loose
skin as she shakes the sleep from her body. The dog rubs
herself against her hip and Philippa sits down to fuss her.
Layla loves the attention, presses her face into Philippa's
hands. Philippa notices scarring and scratches around the
dog's nose, and what look like old cigarette burns.
"Morning."
Philippa turns to Ryan and from just one look he knows
he's in the shit. He sits up and prepares his apologies.

"Don't bother making excuses and stuff," Philippa snaps, and moves away from Layla so she can focus on her anger. "I'm not happy about you staying over, Ryan. It's too soon, for me, anyway."

"I..."

"Let me finish. I like seeing you but I like my own space too and if I say no to something I expect you to be a grown-up and respect that." She feels herself soften somewhat. "But I'm grateful that you were decent enough to sleep on the sofa and not try anything whilst I was out of it."

"I wouldn't, I want our first time, if there is..."

"Oh, God, shut up. Of course there will be. Just not when I'm too pissed to bloody well know what's going on." She lets out a solitary laugh before reining it in and becoming stern again. "But don't you ever smoke in my house again, I fucking hate the smell of it. I mean I didn't even realise you *did* smoke."

Ryan's confused but then he notices the smell himself. He looks around the room as if he expects to see someone standing behind him chain-smoking.

"There's no point in lying."

"I ain't fucking lying!" Ryan jumps to his feet and towers over her for a second before backing off.

"Okay, okay." Philippa defuses the situation. "But you can smell fag smoke too, yeah?"

"Yeah." Their conversation comes to a standstill as neither can explain where the aroma is coming from.

Philippa opens a window and sighs. "But please, don't lie to me, okay?"

Ryan takes her hand. "Babe, I would never do that. I've told you that now and then me and Noggin will smoke a spliff with a beer, but I wouldn't do that around you unless you were into that shit."

"I'm *so* not."

"Which is fair enough, and I totally respect that. But I promise I would never do that in your house." He smirks. "Especially after I decorated it and everything."

She elbows him in the ribs. "Good, 'cause if I catch you smoking that shit in my house you'll be doing it all again, me and Nelly will kick your arse."

"Nelly? Who the hell is Nelly?"

"Oh, I've not told you, have I? This house is haunted by the previous owner, an old lady."

Amusement changes Ryan's face. "Ah, right. Maybe she's the fag hag?"

Philippa gives him a side glance. "That isn't the appropriate terminology, but nice try. No, Nelly's not a smoker, I don't think." She smiles up at the room as though remembering a loved one. "Nelly's a lovely old lady who likes flowers and I have a feeling she has a soft spot for ABBA, too."

Ryan laughs. "You're serious?"

Philippa nods.

"I'm not sure I believe in all that bollocks," Ryan says, becoming sombre, "I mean, my mum did, but you know, she never came back to prove it or anything."

Philippa sits beside him and leans against his shoulder. She likes it when he puts his arm around hers, and Layla's there within seconds. "I never used to believe in that stuff but Niamh reckons she's always seen ghosts ever since she was little."

"Is it her that's told you there's one here?"

"Not as such, no. I've experienced things, atmospheric changes, it comes and goes. It just feels so homely at times, so warm and comforting, motherly, like I'm being swaddled. The house, I mean, being here."

She tells him about the sugar incident and he looks at her like she's crazy. She doesn't give a fuck if he believes her or not as she feels it's real and Niamh is always there to confirm it. Well, she *was*.

She knows how stubborn Niamh can be when she's upset about something, how she'll isolate herself until the hurt has gone or been sufficiently buried for her to pretend everything is fine, but Philippa wants answers. She knows what to do in situations like this, and sends a three-word text message with a code at the end that only they understand, something shared between them as teenagers, symbolising their intense love for one another, a sisterhood that can never be broken.

I love you XXX!

She remembers the accidental exclamation mark after Niamh's three kisses that turned into their secret in-joke. Found it funny how it made those kisses seem more passionate, forceful even.

Thinking about passion and kissing stirs something inside of Philippa that's lain dormant for a long time. She can't remember the last time she had sex, and suddenly nothing else seems to matter, not Niamh, ghosts, or the smell of tobacco that still hasn't left the room. She turns to Ryan, who still looks half-asleep, and asks, "Have you got any condoms?"

Head over Heels

The house is hardly hers before he's in there with her. It's hard for her to pinpoint how it really happened. One night turned into two, then three, and gradually little bits of him are left behind like dirt devils. Toothbrushes, tobacco tins, Rizla wrappers and t-shirts. And Layla. She never wanted Ryan to move in, but she didn't tell him to go, either.

Her friend has deserted her. She has not returned any calls or messages, and after four days of feeling every freckle of her friend's goose-bumped cold shoulder, Philippa bites the bullet and visits her flat. Niamh has gone away for a few weeks, according to her reclusive neighbour, and didn't say when she was returning. Philippa thinks of all the places Niamh might go, could go, and the choices are limitless. She is estranged from her family but has friends all over the planet.

Ryan comforts her, to an extent, and they make the best of what he irritatingly begins to refer to as *their* place. She carries on working, and he calls her each and every break time to fill her in on whatever job he and his mate Noggin are doing and to make sure everything is alright. She notices that the atmosphere of the house has normalised. Gone now is the overly exuberant feeling she'd had whilst she spent the first few weeks alone.

The sensible side of her, no longer blinded by Niamh's fancy persuasions, believes the happiness was simply excitement. No more unusual happenings, aside from an unnatural number of wasp stings and none of the pesky little critters to show for it. She remembers what the estate agent said about there having been a nest in the attic and calls someone to come and investigate. *Bastard things might have come back.* A man arrives and goes over the entire house, attic too, but finds no evidence of infestation. She lights citronella candles on every window sill.

They have their first serious argument the night she receives a text message from Niamh, three-and-a-half weeks after she ran from the house. Layla skulks out in the kitchen when Ryan raises his voice in anger. Niamh's number's changed and the message is brief, no kisses.
I'm sorry, I ran. N
"Who's that?" Ryan asks, another irksome habit to add to a growing list. Those two words barely conceal the sly, untrusting malice behind them that he'll deny if pointed out.
She doesn't answer him, she's too...shocked? Happy? Even that's wrong. An added expletive is now necessary.
"Who the fuck is that?" Ryan reaches out a hand and touches her phone, which causes Philippa's mental dam to break. She snatches her hand away and stares at him.
"What the hell do you think you're doing?"
Ryan brings up some story about his ex-girlfriend, Sharon, who kept secrets and cheated. Philippa tells him her name's not Sharon and if she wanted to cheat she wouldn't be with him. Her reply seems to make him angry; a lot does, she's noticing.

"It's Niamh," she tells him, defusing the situation before it becomes something more. It doesn't, it turns it into another direction, gives his anger a new focus.

"Oh, fucking hell, what's that daft bitch want? From what you were saying, you were better off without her."

Philippa remembers all the things she said whilst she was angry and raging. Angered by her friend's refusal to talk to her. Everything came out of the woodwork then. All of Niamh's dirty little secrets, well, almost all of them, but every little splinter of negativity that was deeply embedded beneath Philippa's skin. The build-up of negativity throughout their lives together. When we're angry we never sing about the good sides of people. But she misses her crazy, witchy sister, her friend who can see leftovers and who would take her back in a heartbeat.

Philippa's adamant that she's going to reply. She does, despite Ryan suggesting that she shouldn't. *Is he worried, or does he just want me all to himself?*

Niamh won't tell her what was wrong that evening, not via a message. It's decided they'll meet the next day, somewhere public in case she makes a twat of herself and starts crying. She puts down her phone and Ryan apologises for snapping and tells her once again his tale of woe, how he was left cheated and heartbroken by the evil Sharon. Philippa forgives him and within thirty seconds his hand is on her breast.

"Not tonight, babe," she says, and kisses him gently on the lips.

Ryan squeezes her again, hard, and there's a look that's a little bit like hatred in his eyes before he tells her, "I'm going outside for a smoke."

Philippa nods and sighs. *At least he doesn't do it in the house.*

A few minutes later the smell of marijuana wafts in amidst the swirls of citronella.

She's My Kind of Girl

It's the first time in forever that she's seen Niamh without make-up and she's lost a considerable amount of weight over the past month. Her cheekbones are more prominent, hard angles that once were beautiful. She even hides her proud peacock hair beneath a woollen hat and Philippa wonders if she's let that routine slip too. When Niamh hugs her she finds it hard to let go and finds it equally hard to stop the tears from forming. The surrounding coffee shop is a blur of colour that doesn't seem to touch Niamh; her vibrancy is gone, she's like a ghost from the silver screen amongst Hollywood Technicolor. Whatever she's going to tell her is going to be bad news. *The* bad news.

Her throat is dry, the coffee doesn't ease it, words grate. "Oh, God, Neem, what is it?"

Niamh doesn't make eye contact, stares into the black depths of her coffee, her despair even; a smile, a skeletal rictus, cracks her gaunt face. "I …I tried to kill myself. Slashed my wrists. The right way and everything, except I didn't go deep enough, or something." Her voice fades.

Philippa can only say, "Why?" Her friend had suffered emotional issues as a teenager but she'd thought all that was sorted.

"I don't want to say," Niamh says, biting at chapped lips.

"Please, Neem." Philippa reaches across, takes her shaking hand. "Come on, it's me. We tell each other everything." Niamh finally looks into her eyes and Philippa can see that whatever she has to say is going to be hard. One of the hardest things she's ever had to tell her, maybe.

"Tell me, Neem. I love you."

Niamh smiles as tears run. "There's something else in your house, Phil, and it *knows*."

No, no, please no. Not now, Neem. Please don't fuck things up for me now. Philippa feels queasy, feels her defences rise like walls. "What's going on, Neem?"

"That night I was last around. When Ryan came to the house."

"What about it?"

"There was a shift in the atmosphere, another presence, something cruel."

"What happened?" Philippa finds her words are cold, she doesn't want to hear what Niamh's saying, doesn't want her home ruined by these fantasies.

Hole in Your Soul

Bad vibes come off this bloke. Niamh's been wrong about people before. Folk have their defences, they put up protective shields that can be interpreted in so many different ways, but she's sure this Ryan is a grade-A dickhead. There's something malevolent in his eyes; the same way some people have a twinkle of mischief, this bloke has a spark of evil. His aura is subdued, dark shades, he wears it like a lion's mane, and, like the predatory cat, he is capable of pouncing at the drop of a hat.

She brushes past him and the stench of pipe smoke and unwashed armpits engulfs her and she finds it hard to comprehend how Philippa can endure such bad hygiene in a partner.

The stench follows her to the toilet, where he's apparently just been, and Niamh's also disappointed in her friend's sudden drop in standards where indoor smoking is concerned.

When she closes the bathroom door and reaches for the window, she notices the shift. The room is full of the man's rancid odour and the atmosphere chokes the air like a house fire.

Niamh backs against the wall between the toilet and the sink; the dizziness of it all, together with her drunkenness, makes her wobble.

Her skin prickles as an unseen presence storms into the room, hot and suffocating.

She wonders if the house really did suffer a fire in the past. She goes to leave the room and then feels a force, stronger than any of the leftovers she's ever come into contact with, thrust her back against the tiles.

A hot hand clamps around her neck; she can feel the rough calluses on the fingers, and forces her chin upwards. "Get off me!" she yelps as another invisible hand clenches her breast. There is nothing to fight against. With immense effort, like walking headfirst into a hurricane, she manages to push herself an inch from the wall, but the hands shove her back, and the one half-strangling her moves below and dives underneath her skirt.

I Am Just a Girl

Niamh closes her eyes and sits back. "I went to the loo and the whole room was freezing and stunk of cigarettes. I thought your bloke had had a cheeky fag and opened the window too late." She pauses and grips her knees to stop her hands from shaking. "I stood to wash my hands, and this force, this *male* force presses me up against the wall and I can smell tobacco, sweat, and feel its breath on me. I can't move. There are rough hands all over me and then..."

"And then what?" Philippa manages to croak.

"And then it throws me to the floor in disgust and I hear a man's voice whisper, *What the bloody hell are you?*"

"You mean...?" Philippa can't bring herself to raise the subject; it's always Niamh's decision.

Niamh nods and laughs bitterly. "Yeah, Casper the not-so friendly ghost did not want to rape a chick with a dick."

One Man, One Woman

Ranga's well fucked off when Philippa comes back from seeing her weirdo mate. She's proper on one, hardly says two words to him. To make matters worse, as soon as she gets home she hides herself away in the bedroom. There are tears in her eyes but if he doesn't notice, he won't have to waste time trying to coax out her problems. He leaves her to it, lets her fester and wallow. Layla joins her; the dog is becoming softer and synchronised with her and they've both packed on some weight these past few weeks. Ranga knows the honeymoon period is well and truly over and he needs to put both his bitches in their place. Her handbag's on the chair and he goes in her purse and takes the solitary twenty-pound note out of it. At times like this, you just need to get some air. And some intoxicating substances in your system.

Angeleyes

Philippa hears the front door slam.

She hides beneath the duvet; the warmth and the smell of Layla are comforting and makes her feel secure. She wraps her arms around the dog, who's not much smaller than her, and they curve into one another, two separate species getting exactly what they need from each other. Her house still feels safe, still feels like hers, so she doesn't understand what's happened. *Has Niamh fabricated something for some reason? Is she having a breakdown? Is she jealous of her and Ryan?* Philippa is concerned about disbelieving her lifelong friend. After all the far-fetched things she has accepted, this doesn't sit right.

What the bloody hell are you?

The mere thought of what Niamh has implied makes her squeeze Layla that little bit tighter. The dog groans with content and slops her chops.

Aren't animals rumoured to be sensitive to such things? Aside from becoming her shadow, Layla is golden. And that overall cosy, safe, blessed feeling she felt whenever she was at home, especially when she was alone at home, *how could that be anything bad?*

Philippa swipes back the duvet and stares up at the dark ceiling. "Hello?"

The house makes noises, subtle creaks, water trickling through the pipes, nothing untoward, but it feels secure.

"Please don't hurt my friend. You might not quite understand her situation. It was probably not heard of in your day. It's just that Niamh was always uncomfortable being a boy, she said it was worse than wearing clothes that didn't fit properly as she had a *body* that didn't fit properly. She's lived this way a long time but nowadays there are special operations that can give people what they want. Help them be on the outside who they are on the inside. Some have the full shebang and have everything surgically removed and altered, some don't but it doesn't matter. It only matters to them and how they feel. They don't even have to do that to be a woman if that's how they feel. I hope you can understand this."

Philippa is surprised that she doesn't feel like an idiot talking to a room, to the house. The temperature seems to go up a few degrees and once again there's the vaguest hint of citrus.

"Thank you," she says, assuming that this atmospheric change is the previous owner's way of acquiescing to her request. "I promise you'll like her if you get to know her."

Layla's eyes flit back and forth across the ceiling and Philippa wonders whether she can see things that her human eyes can't or whether she's listening to the noises of the house.

Philippa pats the dog's head. "Shall we go and get some grub, Layla? We can't stay up here all night, plus I've got to get my stuff ready for work in the morning."

Man in the Middle

"I reckon she's got another man, Nog." Ranga sucks hard on the joint and blows smoke in the air.

"Nah, why would she cheat on you, man?" Noggin says. "Some girls are just like that."

They've been to the off-licence, Ranga's three cans in and he's not sharing. Noggin clings on as though he has no other choice.

"She has some cunt round there when I'm not."

"Yeah?" Noggin asks, "Who?"

Ranga glances at him as if he's nothing. "How the fuck should I know? If I knew, I'd rip the fucker's spleen out, wouldn't I?"

"Yeah, Rang, course."

Ranga rolls his eyes heavenward. "Sometimes, when I've been out, like, I'll come back and there's little whiffs of fag smoke."

"You sure it ain't her? She might have got a crafty habit she's hiding."

Ranga stubs out the joint on the bus shelter window.

"Why are you defending her so much?"

"I ain't."

"It better not be you!" Ranga says, his eyes burning into his friend's.

"Nah, nah." Noggin visibly starts to shake and Ranga loves it. "I wouldn't do that to you."

Ranga keeps staring, just enough to intimidate the man a little bit too much, before cracking a grin and punching him in the arm. "Ah, I know you wouldn't, mate. You're my bro and you know I'd stomp your head in."

Noggin manages an uncomfortable laugh.

"I'll have to make sure I keep my beady eye on her, won't I?"

"Too fucking right. Maybe meet her from work and stuff. She'll think you're being a gentleman and that."

Ranga hands Noggin a can. "Me? A gentleman?" He laughs. "You're a genius, Nog."

"Cheers," Noggin says, smiling shyly. "Err, Ranga, mate?"

"What?"

"Is that barmaid at The Towers, like, available now you and your bird are, like, living together, cuz I've spoke to her a couple of times and quite lik—"

"No, she fucking ain't!" Ranga snaps, and knocks the beer can out of Noggin's hand. It lands on the pavement with a clink and the remainder dribbles towards the gutter. "Got to have some fucking fun whilst the bitch is at work, ain't I?"

Under Attack

Niamh hasn't seen any leftovers since the incident at Philippa's house. She wonders if the gift she's had since birth has faded away.

Philippa's at work but she can hear a dog barking repeatedly. Niamh remembers that the man had a dog; she'd made a fuss of it one time before she went to the bathroom. She stops outside the house. *She's moved him in.* Niamh's hurt that her friend hasn't told her this life-changing news and feels a stab of jealousy. *We tell each other everything!* The dog barks on and on. *Surely if there's someone there they would have made the poor thing be quiet.* The dog lets out a pained whelp and the house seems to bulge with malevolence. The windows darken; she's drawn to peculiar angles and patterns in the brickwork and the rendering for no apparent reason. The normal-looking bungalow reels with a black malice only she can feel. It's the tiger waiting to pounce, the rapist ready to strike. Against all her psychic klaxons, she steps into the small front garden and moves towards the building. It's like walking through a forest fire: the air is heavy, hot with something that really doesn't want her there. She holds her head high in defiance. This is her best friend's house. Philippa is the only other person, aside from her parents, she has ever truly loved. She will not let any harm come to her. If it doesn't want her to come to the house, then she must be able to do something to get rid of it.

The dog screams, it's a weird sound, and there's the scrabbling of claws against the other side of the front door. Niamh crouches and pushes open the letterbox and is greeted with a gust of tobacco and rank body odour. She sees the dog running around in circles, yapping, yelping, and biting at its own body. "Hey, it's okay." She offers it comfort and sees the alarm in its eyes as it hurls itself against the door in a flurry of tooth and fur.

Kisses of Fire

Ryan's there when she comes out of work and her heart melts a little bit at his old-fashioned gesture. "Hello, what are you doing here?" she asks, coyly.

He grins his crooked grin. "Thought I'd surprise you, didn't I?"

"Aw, you're so sweet," she says, and takes his arm. "You should've brought Layla."

Ryan rolls his eyes. "You only want me for my dog."

Philippa neither agrees nor disagrees. "Gotta pop to the shop before we get on the bus, to buy something for dinner."

"Cool, what we having?"

Philippa ignores his presumption, figures that this is just how it is now, although the fear of being in a serious relationship scares her a little. She smothers it with banal conversation. "Something quick and easy."

"Mind if we get a few cans, too?"

"I don't know, babe, I'm a bit short this time of the month."

"Ah, it'll be fine, me and Noggin got a job on tomorrow, I'll be able to chuck you some dosh."

They head into the express supermarket where he makes a beeline to the alcohol aisle and picks up a twenty-four pack.

A few cans? For fuck's sake.

Philippa picks up two Pot Noodles.

He's already cracked the crate open before he's left the store.

"Can't you wait until we get inside?" Philippa says, hating the idea of public drinking.

"Gasping, ain't I?" he says between slurps.

"Evidently so." Philippa, once again, begins to question whether she's doing the right thing by seeing him. He's definitely not the man she thought he was, but now there's the sudden strangeness between her and Niamh, she doesn't know if she can deal with another troublesome splinter beneath her fingernails.

Ryan has obviously detected an atmosphere. He stops centre-pavement, first can already nothing but dregs. "You got a problem with my drinking?"

Philippa is incensed by having to waste money on beer she doesn't want. She's in the mood for an argument. Sometimes when your blood gets up like this you have to seize the moment and let that stuff out of you. Expel those demons. Let rip. And she does. It all comes out. "In fact, yes I do! It's not just every day, it's pretty much all you seem to drink. I don't know how the fuck you afforded it before you met me but I can't keep buying it." She pauses, watching in disbelief as he cracks another can without looking at it. "You invade my personal space, interrupt my time with Niamh under the pretence you were just passing, and try to emotionally blackmail me with the dog."

Ryan knocks back the can in one go but his eyes never leave hers, as though he's waiting patiently for her to finish ranting.

Philippa swings the shopping bag at him, astounded by his lack of reaction. "Oh, and I fucking hate the smell of weed. You smell of stale lager and fags. Fucking have a wash!"

It happens so quickly that she doesn't even register what has happened until she's looking up at him from the path amidst crushed Pot Noodles and her cheek starts throbbing.

"Have your fucking beer!" is all he says, and he lifts the nearly full pack of lager above his head like a rock, his face in simian rictus, and smashes it to the pavement beside her. Cans explode and go off like a lawn sprinkler. Lager soaks into her hair and her laddered tights. Ryan turns tail and storms off into the night. Ludicrously, all she can think about is clearing up the mess he's made.

Put On Your White Sombrero

"Bitch asked for it if you ask me," Keisha the barmaid says, all eyes through fake lashes as she leans across the bar and hands Ranga another free pint whilst the manager's not looking.

Half the beer's gone before he even knows it and he's three-quarters wankered. He nods and test-drives a sentence to see if his words come out slurred. "I just hate being told what I can and can't do."

"You're a man. No proper man would let any woman boss him about."

"Problem is, I was practically living with her. Gave my digs up last week. Ain't told her yet, though."

"Mate, she'll come around," Keisha says, all flirty, "she'd be a fool not to."

Ranga smirks and nods, he's not too pissed to go back to hers. He drops another less-than-subtle hint. "Can't even get any of my stuff. Nog's bloody well started nights at Amazon for fuck's sake. I never thought I'd live to see the day that bloke got a proper job." He flashes the grin he knows she'll not be able to resist. "Fancy letting me walk you home?"

Keisha flushes, the eyelids close for a second too long, and the smile tries hard to be coy. "I know my own way back. I'm a big girl now."

"You never know who's about at this time of the day. Not safe for a pretty young thing like you."

"Go on, then."

It's a dead cert. Ranga knows he can have her any time he wants, gets her type. When he had her naked for the first time, he'd noticed the self-harm marks on the insides of her arms and thighs. She'd gone quiet when she noticed him staring at them, admitted she disliked the way she looked. He told her there was nothing to be worried about, she had an amazing arse and tits. Told her the slash marks were tiger stripes. She liked that. Then he'd fucked the living shit out of her to prove there was nothing physically wrong with her.

He walks her home at midnight. They cut through the cemetery, where he takes note of a fresh floral arrangement on one of the new graves.
Once they're behind closed doors, he's at those heavy tits with his hands and moves in to kiss her.
"You're a cheeky git." She playfully swats at his hand and kisses him hard.
He mauls her buttocks and tells her she's the one with all the cheek. One hand rides up her top whilst the other goes to slide down the front of her leggings. She slaps at his hand properly this time. "We can't tonight. I'm *on.*"
"What the fuck?" he blurts out, and pushes her away in disgust. "You could've fucking told me before I walked you home, you stupid cow."
She's clearly crestfallen. Reaches out to touch his face, and this time it's her hand that's slapped away. "We can still chill out for a bit. Watch a film or something."
Laughter escapes and he revels in the hurt on her face. "Nah, you're alright, I've seen it before."
Keisha stares at her feet; one hand almost automatically begins clawing at her wrist. She looks like a child about to cry. Suddenly her face lights up. "I'll give you a blow job if you want."

Ranga scoffs at her eager-to-please expression. "You're a sad, pathetic, fat bitch." He's destroyed her both sexually and emotionally, and can't decide which is the more gratifying.

"Please, Ranga, I'm sorry." She pines and whines and mewls and crawls as he yanks open the door and once again slips into the night.

On the way back past the cemetery, the effects of the alcohol wearing off, he remembers the flowers and snatches them from the grave, planting a size nine in the overturned soil. He only briefly glances at the headstone, sees it's in loving memory of yet another bitch. Well, that's three he's fucked over in one night, a fucking hat-trick. He chuckles to himself and heads towards Noggin's to share his stash of whatever he's got in.

Slipping Through My Fingers

There's blood and excrement all over her hallway walls and a bus ticket with 'call me, N' written on it in eyeliner. The mess hits her like a blow to the chest. The horrible tobacco smell is back tenfold; it mixes with the rank odour of shit and Philippa feels her gorge rise within the first few seconds of opening the door. She doesn't have time to pick up the bus ticket, hold her hand over her mouth and nose, before Layla rockets towards her from out of nowhere. The dog bounds into her as though she has the devil on her back and she slumps down to the floor in an aching, nauseating pile. Layla isn't trying to attack her, she's covering her face with wet-nosed, needful, sloppy kisses. Her body is covered in red pinpricks, some of which are crusted over with dried blood. Others have been worried and are weeping. Philippa tries to find a patch on the dog where there aren't any lacerations but it's impossible. She hugs the dog close. The skin beneath its short fur is raised; she reads it with her fingertips like braille. Layla, in turn, licks at Philippa's swelling eye, and trembles.

Philippa opens all the windows, empties a can of air freshener, and cleans up Layla's mess. The dog is glued to her side throughout the whole process.

Claw marks have ruined the lacquer on the front door and the carpet looks half-eaten. Closer inspection of the flaking paint reveals at least one claw.

Something seems to have freaked Layla out so much she literally tried to dig her way out of the house. A possible connection with Niamh doesn't cross Philippa's mind until she picks up the bus ticket.

It's a Daysaver, so Niamh must have walked home. Why didn't she text or phone? Philippa takes her phone from her bag and sees that it's dead. *That explains that.*
When the three of them are clean, Philippa, Layla and the house, the shock of the night sucker-punches her in the solar plexus and takes her breath away.

There's an oppressive feeling in her home, as though it's been burgled or violated. She's uncomfortable being naked in her bedroom, feels unseen eyes watching her and hears reruns of Niamh's encounter in the bathroom. Philippa won't get changed in there, it's been sullied by her words even though she's not entirely sure she believes her friend — or whether she *wants* to believe her.
Layla is on edge and will not leave Philippa's side. The dog's triangular head keeps darting towards random corners of the room; a low growl is never far away and the stale tobacco smell still hasn't faded.
When Philippa looks in the mirror to survey the damage, she sees herself with harsh, critical eyes. Focuses on the lines that have slowly deepened around her mouth and on her forehead, the slight dough below her chin that reminds her of her heavier days. She is growing haggard. The bruise is angry-looking but nowhere near as bad as Katherine being so disfigured she killed herself. Philippa counts herself lucky.
Tells herself it could have been worse, that she'd pushed Ryan too far. She shouldn't have said all those hurtful things. She is the one who is in the wrong. No man should be spoken to like that. Women should know their place and she is lucky to have a good-looking young man like Ryan interested in her in the first place. She's a saggy old bitch and should be grateful.

She's warming to the smell of the tobacco; for some peculiar reason, she can even identify the brand, and all of a sudden Layla growls at her and runs to the other side of the room.

"Fucking dog," Philippa grunts, and lies on the bed. The sound of paws scrabbling at the back door makes her sit up and snap. "Cut it the fuck out or I'll chuck you in the canal!"

The dog's desperation for escape intensifies and Philippa storms from her bedroom in a red rage. "Right," she shouts as she leaves the smelly room, "that's it! I'm going to..." But she stops abruptly, forgetting what she was about to do. Away from her bedroom, her house smells how her house *should* smell: hints of vanilla or pine and a subtle undertone of the fruitiness that came with the place. Turning back, she sees her bedroom door bulge as though the darkness within is something solid, tangible. She fusses the dog quickly to try and regain some trust before letting her outside to do her business.

Her sleep is troubled, she doesn't fully wake, but she twists and turns as the thick, cloying odours from the bedroom flow through the house. The dog, too, senses the atmospheric changes, even in her slumber, and pedals her hindlegs in a further bid to escape. Philippa starts to wake but is coaxed back to sleep by a soft, warm hand stroking her hair. Her dreams change to those of childhood and her mother's love.

In the morning, she wakes with a crick in her neck, to the sound of her phone ringing from the bedroom. A beam of sunlight shines on her face and she curses it, imagining herself shrivelling like a vampire. Layla is spread across her waist wearing an expression of contentment.

"Well at least one of us looks like they had a good night."

Philippa rolls the dog off. The house is warm and summery, full of the wonderful feeling that she had begun to associate with the presence of the previous owner.

She smiles and stretches, ignoring her phone and attempting some brief yoga moves to uncrinkle her neck. Her one eye is swollen but the vision is fine. "Alexa," she calls out to the voice-activated speaker aside the television, "play ABBA."

The opening notes of an upbeat number begin playing as she lowers her left ear to her shoulder. "It's always bloody 'Dancing Queen'," she smirks, and rocks her head the other way, massaging the twanged muscle with her fingers. Jasmine-and-orange floods the room and the sun feels warmer on her skin.

Niamh and Ryan have been calling her and there are text messages from both. For a moment she finds it difficult to choose who to speak to first for fear of what either of the recipients have to say.

Niamh wins the contest by ringing again whilst her phone is in her hand.

"Hey."

"Oh, my god, Phil, I've been trying to get hold of you since yesterday afternoon!"

"I'm sorry, Neem, I'm sorry. I had work and my phone died and other stuff happened." With the deliberate way she said the last part, she knows that Niamh will pick up on it.

"What other stuff?"

"Oh, only stuff with me and Ryan." Philippa tries to sound light-hearted but then hears herself splutter the words, "He hit me. I deserved it, I guess."

Although there is silence on the end of the line, she can imagine Niamh's expression. "I'm coming over right now."
"No, I'm fine," she starts, but hears the sound of her friend's door slam right before she hangs up.

Eagle

Ranga is hungover as fuck and smells like a tramp but he's taken the elastic band from Noggin's stack of bills and bunched the flowers into something presentable. It's early, the sun is out, and the day is his. He's confident Philippa will forgive him; it was only a tap anyway and she did give him all kinds of lip, after all, but as he nears the bungalow he makes sure to hang his face and play the part. He hopes his rough exterior will enhance the charade.

A pang of the previous night's anger sparks up again and stabs at the throb of his hangover when he sees a double-decker pull up and her little mate hop off. He slows his pace and stares at the way Niamh's yoga pants cling to her shapely buttocks.

"I'd like to fucking rip them things off you and teach you what happens to snooty, snobby bitches," he mumbles lecherously, out of earshot. He'd love to have a go with a really fit girl like that, one with an athletic body and hair that cost more money than he's ever earned in a year. "I'd fucking destroy you, love."

He watches her pause before going into the front garden, sees her fingers claw at that expensive hair. *She's apprehensive about going in because she's the weirdo who thinks the place is haunted. The one who's putting daft ideas into Philippa's head.* She steels herself and crosses the garden's threshold.

"Fucking nutter." Ranga laughs but still continues to imagine the things he would like to do to her. A line from a film springs to mind, some shite horror that he was only half-watching whilst half-fucked on whatever, and he lets it slur from his mouth in a mediocre impression of the actor. "Yeah, I'd eat the curry out of her asshole."

Philippa opens the door to find that Layla is trying to jump up at Niamh. He shows himself and the dog bolts for him. He uses it to his advantage.

"What the fuck do you want?" Niamh confronts him and stands between him and the doorway.

He looks over her head; not difficult considering how little she is. "Philippa."

"You think some fucking wilted flowers from Asda are going to mend this?" Niamh snaps.

Ranga keeps his face solemn before the gothic pixie and contains his anger for now. "I just want to talk to you." He reaches over Niamh, loving the scent of her perfume, offering Philippa the flowers. "I'm sorry. I can see now isn't a good time."

"Don't you fucking touch her. She doesn't want your fucking flowers, you chavvy piece of shit." Niamh spits at his trainers and then stares in dumbfounded horror as Philippa takes the flowers and smiles weakly. "I'll call you later, Ryan."

Ranga nods, resisting the urge to gloat in Niamh's face, to even let a twinkle of it appear in his eyes.

Everyone looks at the dog.

Layla is in a difficult no man's land, torn between going with him and staying at the house.

"Stay here," Ranga says to the dog, taking a moment to crouch and kiss her on the head. He apologises once more and turns tail. He walks away knowing he'll win Philippa back unless her prying mate interferes too much. Then his thoughts slide back down to their default setting and he gorges himself on thinking about the ways he'd like to interfere with Niamh.

The King Has Lost His Crown

Niamh clocks the way Philippa smiles at Ryan's pathetic offering. "Don't you fucking dare."

Philippa's taken aback. "Dare what?"

"Don't you fucking dare turn into one of these poor deluded women who defends the shitheads that do this."

"I said some really nasty things, Neem."

Niamh grabs her friend gently by the shoulders and looks deep into her eyes. "It doesn't matter what you said, there is never an excuse for this."

"I know, I know, you're right. I'll talk things over with him later."

"You mean you're actually going to speak to the thug after what's happened?"

Philippa nods, and when she blushes it makes Niamh feel sick. "Well, I think I might love him." She rubs a hand across Layla's head. "Plus, I've got his dog."

Oh my god. The dog. Niamh had temporarily forgotten about the dog. She studies the animal, unsure of it after seeing how wild it was yesterday. "Is she okay? I came round yesterday afternoon and you weren't in and Layla was going nuts."

"I think so, but she practically destroyed the place. She's covered in what appear to be stings of some kind."

"Did you leave any windows open?"

Philippa shakes her head. "No, but I keep getting stung by something too." She mentions the pest-control man coming to investigate the matter but not finding anything. Niamh hates to bring up the supernatural despite Philippa's recent encounters, but there's something odd about this house and it worries the hell out of her.

"Layla was trying to get out. She was petrified of something."

Philippa's face falls; she averts her eyes. "It's the leftovers, isn't it?"

They go into the living room. Niamh senses that the house is neutral at the moment, subdued, there are no forces at work. "I haven't seen anything here, if that's what you're worried about."

"Not even in the bathroom?"

Niamh grimaces at the recollection. "No. I think if I had seen something it would have made the experience less scary. It just feels like there is more than one thing here, an incredibly strong, loving, welcoming, positive force and then the polar opposite; something that is full of hatred and anger and wants to see people hurt."

"I think that's what brings the horrible BO and tobacco smell with it. Whenever the house smells like that, I want to curl up and die, and it's more than just the stink, if that makes sense."

"Of course it does. For some reason you're sensitive to what's in this house and I think it's probably sensitive to you, too. I don't quite understand how these things work but I believe that the leftovers can feed off our emotions somehow."

Philippa laughs, and winces when her swollen cheek causes her pain.

"What's so funny?"

"Nothing. It just makes sense. Kind of. How Nelly started playing ABBA on our girls' night in."

"Exactly. If she's the positive vibe in this house then at least she's got awesome taste in music. Maybe you should try and encourage her."

Philippa's laugh turns into a bona fide cackle. "I have images of exorcising the house by playing 'Mamma Mia' on repeat."

"Yes!" Niamh says, brightening. "Cast out the evil one with 'Waterloo'!"

"*Thank you for the music* but fuck off, you lecherous, pipe-smoking bastard," Philippa shouts at the ceiling, and both of them collapse on to the settee. Layla adds a few hearty woofs and joins them for a cuddle.

"But first," Niamh says, making herself serious again, "we need to discuss you and Ryan."

The mood turns sombre at the mention of his name. Philippa adjusts herself and sits up straight. Everything about her mannerisms has changed, it's as if she has a dissociative identity disorder and she's slipped from one persona to the next. Philippa claws at her knees as she sits forward, refusing to meet Niamh's eyes when she talks. "Please, Neem, I don't want to argue about this."

"There's nothing to argue about," Niamh says, and slips an arm around her best friend's shoulders. She knows exactly where this is going, and hates it. Hates Philippa for being sucked in by it. Thought better of the tough girl she'd grown up with and idolised. "You do what you gotta do."

She finally looks at her. "Neem, don't."

"Don't what?"

"Don't try and make me feel guilty."

"I'm not. You know where I stand on stuff like this. You know where you *used* to stand on domestic violence."

"Yeah, but that was before—"

"Before what? Before you became a victim of it?"

Philippa nods silently.

"I can't and won't make you do anything you don't want to do, Pip, but please don't make me sit and watch my best mate go down one of the most destructive, soul-destroying avenues a relationship can take."

"I won't let it happen again." Philippa takes Niamh's hands in hers. "I promise."

Niamh doesn't believe her but has no choice than to accept her words. "So, what were you fighting about, anyway?"

"Money, mostly."

"He doesn't take money off you, does he?"

"No, not as such, but he's forever putting stuff in the basket when we're at the supermarket. Usually beer. He does give me some of the money back when he and his mate do a job for someone."

Niamh can't help but snort. "You make him sound like a gangster."

"I wish. Aren't they usually minted?"

"Not the crap ones." They both laugh at that.

"It's not the money really, aside from the fact that I only take enough out for emergencies or if I need to get something for tea. I always leave my card on the firepl —"

Philippa points to the wooden mantlepiece above the electric fire and jumps up. "It's gone, my fucking card is gone." The mantelpiece is sparse when it comes to clutter, its main function is a nesting place for remote controls and the Alexa speaker. "No, he wouldn't."

Niamh fights the rage boiling up inside again. "Wouldn't he?"

"No." Philippa studies the fireplace and scratches a fingernail along a gap at the back of it. "There's a crack here, it must have fallen down. I'll have to order a new one."

Any idiot can see the fireplace hasn't been moved for years and Niamh hates the levels of denial Philippa is stooping to. She sees that it is fixed to the wall by heavy metal brackets. "You got a Phillips', Philippa?"
"Huh?"
"A crosshead screwdriver."
Philippa finally cottons on.
"Let's pull it back from the wall and see if your card's fallen down behind it."
"Fuck's sake." Philippa groans and goes to the kitchen to locate a screwdriver.

The screws come out quite easily and when they pull the heavy fireplace away from the wall there's a six-inch perimeter of decades-old floral wallpaper.
"Jeez, Mum used to have stuff like that, I've seen it on some of my baby pictures."
"Well, there's dust," Philippa says, and begins to pull out detritus, her hands instantly grey with filth. A plethora of receipts, their details almost erased over time, a random King of Hearts playing card, a postcard, and her debit card. "Got it," she calls triumphantly, and Niamh feels a pang of disappointment.
"May as well get all the other junk out of there." Philippa stretches further into the small gap they've made and unloads the rubbish on to the floor.
"Wow," Niamh says, leafing through the faded receipts, "these are like time capsules. *Our Price*. Remember that shop? I bought a Dido CD single there when I was six."
"Hopefully that's not behind here too."
"Hey, she was an integral part of my childhood. Oh, here's one for Woolworths."

"Yeah, their pick 'n' mix was an integral part of *my* childhood." Philippa sits back against the wall and drops the last of the papers to the floor.

"You and me both," Niamh reminisces. "Remember the unspoken rule we had that if the sweets were already on the floor they were free?"

"Hahaha, yeah, and we used to knock them down on purpose."

"It was fine until Betty Bin Bag caught us."

Philippa snorts and slaps her hands over her face. "Betty Bin Bag. Oh, my god, I'd completely forgotten about her and her scarily huge tits."

Niamh shudders at the memory of the sour-faced Woolworths worker who used to stalk the aisles, her gargantuan breasts sagging and swinging around waist level. "She scared the living shit out of me."

Philippa nods. "I thought she was an actual witch."

They both take a moment to quell the old nightmares before Niamh clutches something between her fingers that makes her gasp.

"What?" Philippa says, scooting over, "What is it?"

A faded betting slip with Thackray's printed across the top. *3pm at Kelso. 13/04/93. This is not YOUR House. 25/1.* A faded pink stamp across it saying 'cashed.'

The intense feeling Niamh gets from the scrap of paper is incredible.

"What is it? What have you found?"

"This," Niamh manages, "*They* had this."

"Huh? What?"

"Whoever lived here. Whoever is *still* here. They both handled this. There's a lot of residual psychic energy coming from this, and it has both of their essences."

Just a Notion

Oh, God, Philippa doesn't want Niamh to start going off with the mumbo-jumbo again, mostly because she's getting closer to believing her every day.

"It's a betting slip," Niamh says, and hands it to her like she's glad to be rid of the thing. "A *winning* slip."

Philippa scans the info and the fading blue biro. "Oh, I think I vaguely remember my dad going in there on Grand National days." She sees the name of the winning horse and a shiver squirms its way right down her spine. "*This is not your house*. How fucked up is that?"

"I know, right?"

Philippa places the betting slip on the pile of archaic receipts Niamh's made, as though it's valuable. "Well, I take it they never won much, considering they died here."

"Who knows? You know how old people can be."

"What makes you think they were old?"

Niamh smiles. "You told me the estate agent said the previous occupant was an old lady."

Philippa had forgotten about that. There's nothing more she can add, so she continues to clear up the mess on the floor. A yellowed business card that's been torn in half catches her eye and she wonders why it wasn't thrown in the bin. *Sparkle Cleaning - Emilia Szymonik*. Just another one of the house's unanswerable mysteries.

Together they push the fireplace back in place and fasten it to the wall, covering up the old wallpaper. Treasure for someone else to find another day.

When she sits back on the sofa, Layla immediately takes her side and Niamh offers to go and make a drink. Philippa watches her friend's enviably slender figure retreat into the kitchen and considers the pact they made when they were kids.

Danny Saughall, with his floppy, curtained hair had broken her heart right before her thirteenth birthday. Philippa was skeptical that one of the most attractive boys in school wanted to take her to the cinema, but it was an act he kept up for weeks, if not months, and eventually she fell for it. Maybe, because he sat near she and Niamh in Art, and had overheard the pair of them chatting, he'd realised there was more to her than her exterior. She gave in. She went to the cinema after starving herself all morning, anything to try and look as thin as possible, only to be greeted by Danny and his gang of amused friends.

"I can't believe you actually fell for it."

His words echoed in her head all the way home and would taunt her for years, but that night, amidst floods of tears, she told Niamh, who had still officially been Neil then. They made a pact that as soon as they were adults, they would live together and be a mad pair of cat ladies. Philippa watches Niamh spin about plucking teabags and spoons, feels the silken warmth of Layla's pelt, and wonders if life would be better without the awkwardness and complications of a sexual relationship. Niamh is single, has always been single, and in this day and age, gender has no bearing on that.

As far as Philippa is aware, Niamh has no desire for a partner of any kind. Aside from the occasional interest in one or two female celebrities, she rarely seems bothered about sex, and it's something they hardly ever talk about. But she's happy, at peace with who she is now and who she plans to be. Aside from the time Philippa attempted suicide, Niamh has never even professed to needing another person in her life. She's an enigma, always has been and always will be. Philippa wishes she could be content like that; curses the way she tends to fall for the arseholes.

The last words Danny Saughall said to her before she refused his existence always replay whenever she goes through relationship bumps. I *can't believe you actually fell for it.* Haunted by a floppy-haired thirteen-year-old who is most likely fat and bald now. Well, she isn't going to fall for it again. If Ryan so much as steps out of line, he's gone. "Fuck you, Danny Saughall."

She looks up towards Niamh again and sees a waft of blue smoke go past her. The strength of tobacco and dirty male engulfs her. "Neem," she whines, terrified as the cloud hovers in front of her and suddenly billows back and rushes at her face, filling her nose and throat and choking her.

People Need Love

There's nothing to do except get wasted. It's the default option for Ranga as he knows he'll probably have the day to himself. Whatever he does and however he does it, it's got to be free as he is brassic.

The offy is run by an Indian family and he knows their routine like the back of his hand. He watches from the bus shelter across the road as a black car drops off the granddad at the kerbside. The granddad shuffles along at a snail's pace in sandals and a knee-length sherwani, beige. He ruminates on this as the old man unlocks the shop. No matter where people are from, they always seem to develop a liking for beige as they reach a certain age. The beige age. The older people get, the less colour they want in their lives, gradually sweating it out of them with every passing year. Ranga vows never to be like that. He gives the shopkeeper a minute after he's flipped the open sign before he enters the shop. Flattened boxes from multipacks of crisps that have long been discontinued line the windows so no one can see in or out. A kettle boils from the doorway behind the counter. The old man pokes his head around the doorpost, adjusting his glasses.
"Good morning, sir."
Ranga nods and walks towards the confectionery.
Three Yorkies and a Mars bar are slipped into his hoodie pockets in the first second.
He's a pro at this, been doing it since he learned to walk. The beauty of it was, the older you got, the more people began to trust you. "Make one for me while you're in there," Ranga calls out. Jovial, friendly banter puts people at ease too.

"You want three sugar?" the man replies, copying his manner.

Ranga smirks as he shoplifts more chocolate. "Nah, mate, I'm sweet enough."

The old man's laughter is infectious, he's alright, a lovely old bloke. A few words from an exotic song sound out as he finds the radio, but by that time, Ranga is already reaching behind the counter for the litre bottles of spirit. By the time the old man is finally at the counter with his coffee, Ranga is through the door and outside.

Ranga checks his phone. Still no answer from Philippa but he doubts there will be until her mate fucks off. It's quarter-past nine and he heads toward the only place there is for him: Noggin's.

When he gets there, he hammers on the door with a fist, knowing full well Noggin will be asleep after doing a night shift at Amazon. He yells through the letterbox. "Come on, you cunt. Open up." The sound of slamming doors comes from within, and eventually someone opens the door.

"Rang, mate?" Noggin stands confused in just his pants. "I thought you were going to your bird's?"

"Yeah, well, you thought wrong, didn't you?" Ranga attempts to barge past, but his bigger friend blocks his way. For a few seconds Ranga is taken aback but then the anger slowly bubbles. "What the fuck you doing?"

"Dude, I've got to go into work."

"So, fucking what?"

"You can't stay here today, come back later." Noggin throws the words out quickly, as though any hesitation will prevent him from saying what he needs to.

Ranga stares up at his friend in disbelief. Shock rapidly overrides the anger until he sees the suspicious fear in Noggin's eyes.

"What the fuck you hiding? If you're holding out on me I'll—"

"I'm not, Rang, I swear, it's just—"

"Then. Let. Me. The. Fuck. In," Ranga barks, and shoves at his friend's naked belly hard enough to knock him aside. Ranga sees the shoes first, little green Converse, far too small for his great ape of a friend.

"Rang!" Noggin calls out from behind him as he rushes up the hallway.

Little Green Converse, a pair of pink socks with sheep on.

"You dirty old fucker," Ranga leers, and makes straight for the bedroom.

"No, Ranga, don't," Noggin shouts, and jogs after him. Ranga bursts into Noggin's bedroom with hopes of catching his shag in the buff. A long, curvy, light brown thigh with added tiger stripes flops from beneath a filthy duvet; Keisha's wide frightened eyes goggle over the top.

Noggin appears behind him in the doorway and before either man knows it, Ranga's fist has connected with his nose and it's spread across his face like a flattened tomato. Noggin crashes into a flimsy chest of drawers and lands on his arse. Keisha screams and backs up against a headboard that's half-embedded in the crumbling plaster. Ranga plants a foot between Noggin's legs and growls at the girl on the bed. "Shut the fuck up, you fucking cunt." He turns back to Noggin and his hands feebly flay in front of his face to ward off any more blows.

"Please, Ranga," Keisha wails, "don't. I love him." Ranga stops then and doesn't realise that he's the one laughing. "You fucking what?"

Noggin gets to his feet and hobbles over to block the way between Keisha and Ranga. "Rang, please, you've got a bird."

Ranga ignores his friend. "How long has this been going on?"

Keisha speaks but she can't look at him. "Two weeks, but—"

"Two fucking weeks!" Ranga twists and punches Noggin so hard in the jaw that he feels something give and he reels sideways, back into that chest of drawers, which he hits with his forehead and slaps to the floor.

Keisha is back to screaming when she sees the gash that's opened up above Noggin's eyebrows—and the blood that begins to flow freely from it.

"Oh, my god, what have you done?" She claws bunches of duvet to her chest.

Noggin is on the floor, bleeding heavily into the carpet. He isn't moving but his eyes are open.

Ranga will not let his fear rise to the surface. He glares accusingly at Keisha and points at Noggin. "Look. Look at what you've done by opening those fat thighs to everyone in town."

"I—"

Ranga notices Noggin's chest going up and down and breathes with relief. "See? He's fine. The cunt."

It doesn't seem enough, what he's done. Whilst he doesn't know whether he's happy or not that his friend is alive, what he has done doesn't seem to be enough. The thing that angers him most is that he believes them. Believes that there are actual feelings there. Noggin was always a soft fucking twat, and girls are *all* soft fucking twats.

Rage burns inside him so fucking much he imagines flames shooting out when he talks, as though he's a dragon of fury. Noggin's eyes track his pacing but he still doesn't move. Ranga closes his eyes against the red in front of them and when he opens them he calculates exactly what kind of retribution this deserves. He looks long and hard at his immobile best friend and then whips the duvet from the bed to expose the vulnerable naked girl beneath. He ignores every single one of Keisha's screams as he unzips his pants and says to Noggin, "There's no such thing as love."

On and On and On

Niamh turns when Philippa calls her name. She sounds like a little girl. Just before something happens, Philippa is rigid on the sofa, fingers digging into the tops of her thighs. Then she recoils, mouth wide open. Niamh doesn't do the clichéd thing of dropping the teacups to the linoleum but she does throw them towards the sink in an explosion of scalding liquid and porcelain.
Philippa has her hands over her face; her uninjured eye bugs out in fear or pain, she gags and chokes.
Niamh pulls Philippa's hands away from her face to see what has happened but her friend slips from her grasp and claws at her throat in panic.
"Phil, what's wrong?" To begin with, there is nothing to see aside from her distress, but then Niamh sees little marks like splinters freckle the skin around her lips. Philippa opens her mouth and Niamh sees her rapidly swelling tongue. Niamh hits triple nine on her phone and clutches Philippa's hands as she waits for the call to connect. "Try and calm down," she says, knowing full well it's a stupid thing to say.
"Something. Stuck." Philippa coughs but is able to take shallow breaths through her nose.
"It's going to be okay," Niamh insists, and gives details to the emergency operator.

Once the adrenaline has kicked in and Philippa's breathing becomes more regular, the paramedic studies the lesions on her face and looks around the room towards the windows.

"So, where did the stripey little buggers go?" He faffs around with the medical apparatus that's still connected to Philippa.

"What?"

The paramedic, plump, balding, and in his fifties, smirks at their perplexed faces. "Wasps. I bloody hate the things."

"What have wasps got to do with anything?" Niamh asks, not in the mood for this man's upbeat personality.

He points a latex-covered finger at Philippa's face. "The marks, they're wasp stings. You're lucky they didn't leave any stings behind. I had a patient last summer who disturbed a nest and–"

"There weren't any wasps!" Philippa begins but catches Niamh's expression and thinks about the previous marks she's found on herself and Layla, and remembers what the estate agent told her.

When the paramedic has left, but not before providing her with what-to-do-if instructions, Philippa tells Niamh about the wasps' nest.

"Are you sure you didn't see anything?" Niamh asks, staring at the ceiling as though she has x-ray vision.

"There was nothing there, only smoke or vapour."

Niamh laughs and shakes her head. "Ghost wasps."

"We don't even know what ghosts are. Whether they are leftovers from our emotions, our souls, or something else like time lapses, history repeating itself, imprinting itself on the present."

Philippa waves Niamh's words away. "Oh, God, don't go giving me a lecture, Neem, what the hell do I do about this shit? I don't want to move."

"We could try burning some sage?" Niamh suggests.

"Have you got any sage?"

Philippa starts to shake her head but then chirps up with, "I think there's a box of sage-and-onion stuffing mix in the kitchen."

"I'm being serious, Phil. This house needs to be saged."

"Jesus, sometimes you are so full of shit. How the hell is setting fire to herbs going to help this matter? Fucking get the ghosts stoned or something?"

"I'll have you know there are many benefits of burning sage. Aside from the spiritual stuff like cleansing negative energy, if there is any, and empowering objects, it's really good for ridding the places of air pollution, mould, dust, germs." Niamh scrunches one of Layla's ears. "And it's a natural insect repellent."

"Okay, and if that doesn't work?"

"We get a Ouija board or you move out?"

"I'm not going anywhere," Philippa says stubbornly, "I love this house."

Niamh nods. "We just need to find out what the hell's up with the negative stuff. Look, maybe you should come and stay at mine for a couple of nights. I don't think it's safe here."

Tears begin to surface. "No, no. I won't be driven out of my home by this shit. It's not fair. It's not their house anymore. It's mine." She moves to the middle of the room. "Did you hear me?" she screams. "This is not your house anymore, it's mine!"

They both wait. It feels as though the house is listening.

"Go on," Philippa whispers, "do something else. I dare you."

"Pip, you really shouldn't—"

"Do something!"

Nothing happens apart from the silent anticipation.

"I didn't think so," Philippa scoffs. "You're going to have to come up with a lot more than wasps and wafting weird smells under my nose to get me out of here. I'll wear a beekeeper's uniform if I have to."

"Phil, don't antagoni—"

"No, this is my house. And that bastard is trying to drive me out. I'm going to find out who he is and get rid of him."

"Him? Who?"

"The one who reeks of pipe smoke and sweat. It's so obvious it's a male presence. You said yourself you heard a man in the bathroom."

"That doesn't mean the negative energy is male."

"Of course it is, I can feel it and so can you. And it's one of the worst kinds. Dirty. Filthy. Jealous. Bitter." She's spitting the words at the walls, at the fireplace and the window. "Abusive."

Niamh hears the slap of skin and sees the unblemished side of Philippa's face redden.

"You always were a coward!" Philippa shrieks, sounding like someone else entirely. Niamh stands open-mouthed, agog with horror.

`Hasta Mañana

Ranga's heart is racing. This is worse than anything he's ever done. *Shit. Shit-shit-shit.* The red anger inside him is all-consuming, overriding that almost non-existent part of him that knows when to stop. *They fucking deserved it*, he tells himself over and over, but it won't erase the expression of utter desolation on Keisha's face as he did what he did; as she reached out for her lover who lay bleeding from the head. Racist slurs swirl around in his head, added to the already vicious thoughts he's having, stuff that seemed alien to him before. He used to be a city kid, grew up with kids of every nationality and every skin colour. He didn't think like that. And yet the anger that swells inside of him now pulses with outdated insults and views he has never considered. *They still deserved it, though.*

An ambulance rushes past in the direction of Noggin's place and he quickens his step. "Fucking left my shit there." He pictures his booze and chocolate on Noggin's bookcase. Now that was a regular thought.

He needs somewhere to lie low but there isn't anywhere. He has no money and what little stuff he did have is in boxes at Noggin's or at Philippa's. He's being washed down Shit Creek rapids and there's nothing left to cling on to.

When he closes his eyes he can see Noggin's face pressed against the floor. He looked just like he did the very first time they met, except then his face was being pressed into the concrete of the playground by Gary Butcher for being the only black kid in their class.

Gary fucking Butcher.

Ranga hates his mind for dredging this shit up, wants something to numb it. Gary Butcher ended up jumping from the Ramford Road railway bridge when he was nineteen. Noggin and Ranga had a party. *Good riddance to the cunt.* That day in the playground, he'd barrelled into Butcher like an express train. Noggin and Ranga had been inseparable ever since.

And now you've gone and fucked it all up, lost your only friend.

"Nah, he'll come round. He'll see that that tart is to blame. Giving it to everyone who asks." Ranga argues with his conscience, confident he can get Noggin to forgive him. He'll leave it a few days, somehow get a stash and go back there with his tail between his legs.

That's if you haven't killed him.

The thought chills him and now he's the one who feels like a frightened schoolboy with his face being crushed against the tarmac.

Oh, Christ, what if I've killed him?

The streets go past unnoticed as he treads a weary path that has no destination. The skies have clouded over and it's going to rain. There are two boys in the bus shelter blaring out tunes on a mobile phone. He sees the bus ticket in one of their hands, and, ever the opportunist, seizes the moment. Without breaking stride, he snatches the square of paper from between the lad's fingers.

"Oi! Fuck off," the lad cries out, but makes no attempt to retrieve the stolen ticket. There's fear in his friend's eyes. Ranga checks the ticket is an adult one and growls, "Piss off."

"Come on, man," the boy pleads, "I need to get home."

Ranga stares hard at the youth and doesn't have to say another thing. They scoot off and when they're at a safe distance, shout abuse. He takes one step in their direction and they scram. A bus looms in the distance and Ranga sticks his thumb out.

Move On

"What the hell was that?"

"What was what?" Philippa asks, afraid that something else has happened that she hasn't detected.

"It was like watching someone switch personalities. You totally went weird then." Niamh's face is etched with concern.

Philippa was aware of her rant at the forces in the house but the words that flowed from her were beyond her control; like talking nonsense in her sleep but still being privy to it. It's not the first time it's happened, either. "I …" she begins, the knowledge just coming to her, "spoke like I knew who I was talking to, didn't I?"

Niamh nods. "I think they're trying to work through you." The implications are both frightening and ludicrous. Words such as 'possession' spring to mind and Philippa conjures up a montage of clips from the worst horror films. She remembers the other day when she said evil things about Layla. It's as if there are two spirits continuing their life of domestic violence and using her as the conduit. "Shit, Neem."

Niamh rests a hand on Philippa's knee. "It's okay, we'll figure something out. You can come and stay at mine for a few days, it'll be like the good old days when we used to have sleepovers."

"Yeah, okay. I better message Ryan to come and get his stuff and Layla."

"Want me to be around for that?"

"No, it's something I need to sort on my own. I'll come to you after."

Now Niamh's gone, she feels on edge. The walls seem too close to her peripheral vision and she feels alone. Isolated. A lot has happened in the last day. Being hit and swallowing a wasp, they were physical things. She can't accept that there are ghosts of bloody wasps in her house, it's hard enough for her to acknowledge that there is anything paranormal going on at all. Her rational side tries to offer explanations, even points fingers at Niamh's influence. There is nothing she can do until she has seen or heard something more tangible, and even then, unless it is witnessed by another person, she will doubt her own mind. There is something, though, a feeling in the place that usually leaves her feeling high or low.

Enough of thinking about this. she tells herself, mentally checking for any weird vapours and instinctively going to cover her mouth; she even considers hunting for the Covid masks she'd bought in bulk.

Layla's presence reminds her that she'd got rid of Niamh so she could make Ryan come and get his dog.

"Alexa," she says, loathing the silence now that Niamh has gone, "play ABBA."

The voice-activated device on the mantelpiece starts playing a song she's not familiar with, but it's clearly the right band.

This should brighten the place up; she wonders if the ABBA thing could actually be something psychological to do with her.

Thinking of the band and their music triggers happy childhood memories. There are a few other bands that have similar effects: Queen, The Beatles, The Rolling Stones. Bands she'd grown up listening to. Happy times. What if she was somehow projecting these feelings and phenomena? She was more willing to believe that than the idea of spirits.

Enough.
She texts Ryan and takes some painkillers for her eye and throat.

No Doubt About It

Ranga's on the bus when he gets her message. She's lucky she sent it when she did as his battery is only on twelve percent.

You need to come and get Layla.

That's it, then. He's going to have to pull out the big guns now or she'll slip through his fingers too.

He jabs a thumb against a stop button and makes his way to the front of the bus. He gets off in the industrial estate and immediately crosses the road to wait for a bus back. It's quiet around, everyone's at work or at home, rather convenient for what he's about to do. There's a warehouse near the bus stop, he hasn't a clue what it's for and he doesn't care. He runs over to it and smashes the side of his face along the coarse brickwork. It hurts. Checking that no one has seen him, he beats at the wall with his fists, not stopping until his knuckles are bloody. In the reflection of his mobile phone, one side of his face is striped with grazed skin; it reminds him of how Noggin looked that day in the playground. He jogs back to the bus stop, knuckles dropping, just in time for the 56 to come around the corner.

The driver looks worriedly at the state of him as he steps onto the deck.

"I've just been attacked! Help me!"

The bus driver acts like it's a major inconvenience, glances around outside the bus in case it's an elaborate kind of ambush, but he's got a vehicle full of passengers and already a couple of jewellery-laden girls have abandoned their prams to come to Ranga's aid. He gets out of the cab and finds a wad of tissue for him. The young mothers mollycoddle Ranga and he offers them his award-winning smile as they tend to his wounds.

Rock Me

Niamh gets back to her one-bedroom flat and gets to work making sure it's spick and span for Philippa to stay over. She's not been to this place yet and there's a slight apprehension about showing off so little a space. Above her sofa is a huge mural of photographs dating back to long before her birth and Neil's. She doesn't hide her past away but isn't frivolous with what she tells people. The only people she still knows after her transition, aside from one or two extremely loyal friends, are family. It's a wall loaded with so many memories that she often watches it rather than the television. From pictures of a chubby blonde pre-teen Philippa sat on a tree branch beside Neil in his oversized tie-dye and Alanis Morrissette hair to thinner pictures of both of them, older, feeling a lot more like themselves. Dresses, cocktails, sun, beaches, grass. Niamh knows, deep down, that she's kind of been in love with Philippa from the day they met, but she also knows she's waited twenty years too long to say anything. The feeling has evolved into something beyond physical attraction and love. She feels, when she's with Philippa, that they are a pair of old grandmothers, or maybe aged lesbians, that the physical side of their relationship has been and gone and there is that much peace and harmony and comfort in one another's company there isn't any need for that kind of intimacy. They are as close as lovers, in tune as though they've been together for millennia.

Niamh flicks through her books on spirituality and reacquaints herself with the ways to cleanse houses of unwanted presences. All houses should be purified when they take on new owners. It's not simply a case of painting and decorating and tending to repairs. Sometimes that's akin to covering bruises with makeup and pretty garments when the person beneath is a victim of all kinds of abuse. Whoever lived in Philippa's house before, and Niamh suspects the elderly lady, cherished that place. It was more than just a house to her; it was something deeper than bricks and mortar. Maybe it had been in her family since it was built, or her own parents had lived there? But to that person, this house was their church and the aftermath of their joyous celebration and worship could be felt even after their death; the repercussions were still rippling. Then there is the negative energy, be it a traumatic incident that has imprinted itself in the building or the leftovers of someone sinister. If Philippa will agree to it, she'll perform a séance, or at least try to. It's been a long time since she last attempted such a thing but she will do it for her best friend. She thinks about the hands that grabbed at her when she was alone in the bathroom and the disembodied voice that hissed its disappointment at finding out she wasn't exactly what she appeared to be, and she's determined to rid the place of that entity before it tries the same thing with Philippa.

Ring Ring

"What the fuck, Ryan?" Philippa opens the door. She lets him in, hands wrapped in bloody blue tissue, half of his face a red mess.

"It's what I fucking deserve," he shouts, tears cleaning the blood from his cheek.

"What the hell happened?" Layla rushes past her and Ryan falls to his knees, wraps his arms around her, and buries his face in her fur. The dog looks at Philippa with concern as his body shakes with sobs.

Philippa gets on the floor with them and puts an arm around his shoulders. "What happened, babe? Who did this?"

Ryan pulls away from the dog, his face covered in fur and blood, his eyes bloodshot. "It doesn't matter. I fucking deserve it."

"Nobody deserves this. What happened?"

Ryan slumps against the wall. "I slept rough last night." He looks like a little boy.

"Where?"

"In the cemetery."

"That's where the flowers came from, isn't it?" Philippa can't help but smirk.

Ryan nods. "Yeah."

"Did someone mug you or what?"

"No. This happened just before you messaged me. I... you mustn't say anything." Ryan's eyes widen with fear.

"I won't."

"I went to Noggin's, to get my stuff."

Philippa frowns. "Why was your stuff at his?"

Ryan bangs his head against the wall and the tears resurface. "Cuz I'm a stupid cunt. That's why."

"Yes. Yes, you are, but that still doesn't really explain things."

Ryan studies his wrapped knuckles. "We were getting on really good."

"Yeah, we were."

"And I was staying over all the time."

"Yeah. And?"

"I gave up my flat because I hoped that..."

"Hoped that what?"

He hangs his head. "I hoped that you'd say yes and we could live together."

Philippa chokes on the laugh that tries to escape. "Say yes to what, Ryan?"

"I know, I know. I hit you. I'm sorry. I've never done that to a woman before in my life, I swear."

"Say yes to what, Ryan?"

"To marrying me." He looks ashamed when he says it. "I know I did what I did and there's no excuse —"

"No, there isn't."

"The things you said, about my drinking and stuff, well, they're true, but it hurt like hell to hear you say them. I need help, Phil, I want to be a better man. I hoped I could do that with you."

She's on the verge of tears herself. "Why —" She waggles a finger at his face.

"I told him what I did —"

"And he hit you for that? Good. Good on —"

"No. He doesn't give a shit about stuff like that. I told him how I felt about you. My intentions, like, and how I wanted to quit the booze and weed completely."

"And he did this because of that?"

"You don't know what he's like. He's a control freak. Isn't happy unless everyone owes him something. He said I should embrace the fact that we had split up and get on with my life."

"So why don't you?"

"Because you're all I want. I'd give up anything and everything for you. I love you."

Her barriers break and there's nothing she can do to stop the tears and the smile. "I think, for some insanely stupid reason, that I love you too."

Ryan reaches out and she grips his swaddled hands.

"Marry me, Phil, please?"

It's the first time anyone has asked her and she is so overwhelmed with excitement and emotion that she blurts out a high-pitched *yes.*

They fall into each other and her mind is a jumble. *He smells, smells so bad, but it's okay because he's admitted he has a problem and he's promised to get it sorted out and, oh my fucking god, he's asked me to marry him. Someone has asked Fat Philippa to marry them. Hold the bloody front page. Hold. It.* She visualises their new life together, five decades mapped out in five seconds, and it's beautiful.

Should I Laugh or Cry

Niamh's on an armchair with her mobile phone, loud speaker on. "And you said yes?" There's no mistaking the venom in her voice.

"I know what you're thinking," Philippa starts, but there's no way she does.

"You do?"

"You're thinking I'm stupid because he hit me."

"Amongst other things."

"I know it's too early to plan things, and Ryan has definitely got to prove himself after this, I know that, I really do."

Niamh knows from past experience that her friend will follow her own path to its hazardous end despite the danger signs. "Look, I just want you to be happy and certain."

"I know, Neem, and I want you to be happy for me. I can't do this without you."

Philippa's reliance is both a burden and a blessing. Whilst every one of her heartbreaks is felt, deeply, as though they are conjoined twins, Niamh can't bear to live without her friend. Seeing Philippa with other people doesn't sting like it used to but seeing her with the wrong people hurts like stomach cancer. "You know I'll never leave you." Niamh breathes the words so quietly she half-hopes Philippa won't hear.

"I love you," Philippa sniffles.

"Love you too," Niamh croaks, then clears her throat of the emotion. "If he hits you again I will kill him, okay? That's a promise, not an idle threat."

Philippa laughs the tears away.

"I'm not joking, Phil. I'll rip his balls off and make him choke on them, I swear to God."
"Jeez, Neem, okay."
Philippa still thinks she's joking but Niamh knows without a doubt she would kill for this woman. The easy option would be to vanish from her life altogether. Disappear, mourn, and get over the loss of a lifelong friend, but she knows she can't and hates her own dependency. The conversation has reached the lowest point and it's up to her to do what she's always done and force a smile to her face, a song to her voice. "Well, it goes without saying that I'm going to be the Maid of Honour, and I'm going to be the one who organises the hen do."

Take a Chance on Me

Since the spontaneous marriage proposal his brain has been alive with thoughts and ideas that don't even seem like his own. Bullshit flows from his lips more freely and convincingly than ever before. The next roll in his game is cast.

It's pretty much all lies but there's no way either of them can find out the truth. Ranga's got the pair of them sussed, knows that the way to completely win Philippa over is through her fitty of a friend. He encourages Philippa to make her come around so they can get to know each other properly, clear the air of all the nasty shit that's happened. It's a brave move, and he's proud of himself. Ranga knows everything there is to know about substance dependency, you don't just go cold turkey. Whilst they're on their own, he craftily worms his words so that it's Philippa who suggests he cuts down on the booze and weed to begin with, with the intention of cutting it out completely.

He's actually surprised her mate had been so eager to come back once she'd heard about his proposal but he reckons it's to keep an eye on them, well, him especially. *She can keep an eye on me all day*, he thinks, as they awkwardly take their seats around the coffee table.

His knuckles have scabbed over and he resists the urge to pick bits off, has to be on his best behaviour. The innocent little schoolboy must come out to play. "I think it all started with my parents," he says, looking at his fingertips, "they were both pissheads and used to lay into each other pretty much all the time."

Niamh sits impassive whilst Philippa takes hold of one of his hands.

"And obviously, I hated seeing my dad leather my mum and used to get involved." He pauses, allowing Niamh to add some snide remark about him following in his father's footsteps, but she doesn't. He knows she's thinking it, though, they both are. He's wise to that shit. "It's my one biggest fear," he says, allowing a subtle tremor to flutter through the vowels and consonants, "to grow up and be like him. Like my bastard of a father." Tears come, Philippa comforts, Niamh's evidently seen better acting. "It's why my mum drank, because of that wanker, it's why I started. He encouraged it. Told me it's what men did. Was always worried about me growing up queer." He notices a change in Niamh when he says that, she sits up, more focused, adjusts those amazing legs of hers. *Ah, social warrior, are you? Into all that LBQTA or whatever the fuck it is. I know where you're at now, bitch.* "I mean, there was a time, when I was a teen, where I thought I might have been, you know."

"Been what?" Niamh asks abruptly.

Ranga contains a smirk. "Queer. Or at least, you know, bisexual. But I knew if I had said anything to my dad he would have killed me."

She scrutinises him, her eyes bore into his as though she's a human lie detector. He holds her stare.

Ranga's impressed with himself; he's definitely hit a button here, so he decides to push it further, just a little. "When I was fifteen there was this boy," he says, being sure to leave another dramatic pause for effect, he's got the pair of them right where he wants them now, and no mistake, "Ricky Jameson." *Ricky Jameson.* He congratulates himself on a kosher-sounding, completely made-up name. "My mum caught us messing around in my bedroom and threatened to tell my dad if she ever saw so much as one more hint that I was that way inclined."

Niamh's severity begins to falter and he feels he's losing her.

"He killed himself a year later," Ranga adds quickly, killing off the non-existent person. "Nothing to do with me. Drugs."

Philippa squeezes his hand; at least she is still hooked.

"The thing is, I know what my faults are. I know where I've gone wrong. And obviously, when you hear that shit from someone you fucking idolise, it breaks your fucking heart. I'm sorry, I really am. I'm sorry to both of you." He clasps Philippa's hands. "To you for hurting you, using you." He takes a deep breath and turns to Niamh. "And to you, for coming in between you and your friend, for you having to see her hurt like that. I'm sorry. I'll do whatever it takes to prove it to you, I swear."

Oscar-winning performance, that.

Ranga frowns slightly when the old man's voice appears in his head like a thought, and wonders which shadow of his chequered past has come to haunt him. On the cusp of his olfactory senses he detects the faintest hints of pipe smoke and thinks for a second of Philippa's ghosts.

If It Wasn't for the Nights

They're watching something on Netflix when it happens.
With Ryan there all the time, the bad feelings have slowly
started to dissipate and they nestle into a taster of marital
life. He surprises her in the early days by signing up with
an employment agency and starting work immediately.
His shift conveniently finishes just before hers and he
meets her from work every day like a true gentleman. His
addictions are harder to battle but they're out in the open
and he seeks medical advice to kick them.

She knows that together they can do this.

They're snuggling on the sofa, Layla sandwiched between
them. The dog distracts them from the flatscreen on the
wall, she's jiggling and gyrating in her sleep and making
low, grumbling noises.

Chasing rabbits.

That's the sort of thing Philippa's parents used to say.

She wonders what modern day town dogs chase in their
dreams, Hermes delivery men and rolling nitrous oxide
capsules?

They take it in turn touching the dog's face lightly and
laughing quietly at her reactions but then things take a
turn for the worse.

Layla goes rigid as though she's having some kind of seizure. Her third eyelids are meaty red slivers, slash marks on her cheeks. Instinctively, Philippa places a hand on the dog's chest. Layla springs awake, and in an addlebrained state of confusion clamps her jaws down on Philippa's arm. Her immediate reaction is to try and pull away but Layla bites harder. It hurts like holy hell but Philippa doesn't think Layla's pierced the skin yet.

"Layla," she says firmly, hoping to rouse the dog from her sleep terror, but Ryan swings a fist which lands smack-bang on the end of her nose. Layla snaps awake, her huge mouth opens to wail, and she falls off the sofa.

"What the fuck?" Philippa can't choose which hurts more, her arm or Ryan's reaction. Layla's running around, dazed.

Ryan scoots forward and roars at the dog, more aggression on his face than Layla has ever shown. Layla cowers and scarpers into the kitchen.

"What the fucking hell did you do that for?"

He looks at her in surprise. Surprised that she's not fawning over him for being her hero. "You have to get primal with them when they're like that. It's the only language they understand."

"You bloody decked her!" She rubs at her arm; the skin isn't broken but there are clear indentations.

Ryan sucks in air through bared teeth and jumps to his feet, hands rubbing over his fuzzy ginger scalp. He closes his eyes and takes deep breaths, something he's started doing to control his anger. He takes deep breaths and lets them out, trying his best to remain calm.

His first five words are strained; she can hear that he's giving it his all to quell the rage within but he spits out a single profanity which is a snippet of his bottled-up fury.

"I was worried about your fucking arm."

"You don't treat animals like that. Or people." She regrets adding the last bit, they had already agreed not to bring *that* up again. Ryan turns his back to her, head hung, shoulders rising and falling, hands opening and closing as he breathes through his anger.

She's about to apologise for bringing up the forbidden topic when there's a loud bang that startles them both. It takes a few seconds for her to find the source, a lightening crack across the television. Did he headbutt it? It's the only logical solution. But he hasn't moved, she's been watching his every mannerism for signs he was controlling the beast within.

"Oh, fucking nice one, you've ruined the telly, now," Ryan says, stepping aside to show her the damage. "Your phone, too, probably." He laughs at her. "Maybe you should try some of these breathing exercises." He storms towards the front door. "I'm going for a walk. Layla, come on." The dog pokes her head around the passageway on the other side of the dark kitchen. Ryan shrugs.

"Whatever. Leave you bitches to sulk together." Continuing his path out, he grumbles, "Don't come crying to me if she rips your face off."

He closes the door quietly, calmly, but Philippa's still caught up in the shock of it all.

The oppressive feeling is back in the house now she's alone, and she stares at the distorted image on the TV screen in confusion. Her mobile phone sits in two halves amongst the mantelpiece paraphernalia. As she waits for the familiar old-man smells to surface she wonders how the hell she's going to be able to pay for the damage.

You Owe Me One

Breathe through the anger.
Breathe through the anger, my fucking arse. Ranga heads
straight towards the nearest pub. At least if he gets back
pissed, he can blame it on her this time.
Nothing wrong with a lad wanting a drink, son.
There it was again, the old man's voice come to haunt his
thoughts.
It must be my dad.
Ranga thinks about his father, how he practically lived at
the pub. Drinking and smoking— the stuff tasted like shit
but was something he'd had to do. As a kid, Ranga had
never understood it, but he does now. *They drive you to it.*
It's true, women always drive you to do the wrong things,
the bad stuff, whether it's because you're pining after a
particular bird or just any at all, or whether it's once you
find one, they constantly nag at you and try to
domesticate you like a fucking animal. He's the alpha
dog, a fucking wolf, and if he can't break free of the chain
she has around his neck, he'll end up ripping her throat
out. *You've just got to show her who's boss.*
Too fucking right, but it's hard with these modern women.
Philippa is a lot stronger than he has given her credit for
and a large part of him regrets getting into her pants.
You're scared of her.

"No, I'm not!" Ranga blurts out, making a group of lads smirk at the weirdo talking to himself. But his dad has hit the nail on the head. For the first time in his life, Ranga has met a woman he can't control and has made the ridiculous mistake of proposing to her. He has a vision of an older version of himself doing husbandly chores like putting up shelves and hosting barbecues for other couples. The proposal was a spur-of-the-moment thing, something to get him out of a tight spot. And into a fucking tighter one.

Ranga quickens his pace, doesn't like the way his head is working, is worried that this recent audio manifestation is something other than his subconscious.

I Still Have Faith in You

She picks up the pieces of her broken phone and studies the cracked TV. "Fuck." They're both insured for accidents but how she's going to explain her phone colliding with the screen is another thing. Philippa presses the busted handset to her ear. "Er, hello, does your insurance cover poltergeist activity?" The realisation that that was most likely the cause of this incident infuriates her and she turns to the room. "You piece of shit. What the fuck do you want from me?"

Unlike the last time she'd spoken directly to the presence — or presences — within her home, nothing happens, there's no palpable atmosphere, the house breathes normally. "What's the matter? Cat got your tongue?"

More and more she wants Niamh to try and make contact. She's desperate to communicate with it, with them, to know that she's speaking directly to them, even if it's just to tell them to fuck off.

Layla senses it first, her nose twitches before orange-and-lemon floods the room like an automated odouriser. She feels her mood begin to brighten, her pessimism transforming into optimism, and she knows it isn't genuine. "Oh, no you don't." Philippa waves her hands through the air to clear the smell away. "Where the hell were you when my phone was flying through the air?"

Niamh's right, both good and bad presences are feeding off her emotions, Ryan's too, more than likely. Hell, even the dog isn't safe. "Why the fuck don't you do something other than try to make me feel all safe and cosy? Because, do you know what? I don't. I'm starting to seriously consider moving and leaving this place to rot." The citrus intensifies but then rapidly fades. "What, no fucking ABBA, Nelly?" Philippa scoffs and buries her face in her hands. When she lowers them, there, right in the centre of the coffee table, are the two halves of the yellowed business card she'd found behind the fireplace, the card she *knows* she had thrown away. The card that most definitely wasn't there a second ago.
Sparkle Cleaning - Emilia Szymonik.

Crazy World

"Okay, okay, Phil, calm the fuck down." Niamh can barely understand half of what Philippa's saying. For some reason she's phoning her on her archaic landline and it's crackly as fuck. "Why the hell are you ringing me on your home phone? The reception's shit, I'm, like, getting one in three words."

"Something happened."

"Something happened? Okay, I got that bi—" Niamh temporarily freezes. "Did he hit you again?"

Painstakingly, Niamh manages to get the information from Philippa.

"You threw that card away, didn't you?"

"Yeah, weeks ago."

Niamh smirks but feels suspicion bubble up like indigestion. "You're not having me on, are you?" She hates having to ask, but she can never accept that Philippa believes in the supernatural, and hearing her admit to what sounds like an incident of poltergeist apportation is a lot to take in.

"Neem—" Philippa whines, sounding offended before yet more crackles disguise her next words.

"It's the fourth stage in poltergeist activity." Niamh tries to hide her excitement and can't help but think of Egon in Ghostbusters.

"I don't give a flying fuck about what activity they're getting up to. What do we do about the card?"

"Call the number on it? I mean it's probably not in use now but it's worth a try, isn't it?"

Niamh leaves her friend and her dodgy phone line to decide whether to call the cleaner, and mentally leafs through her knowledge of poltergeists. Stage four is a rare stage that doesn't necessarily manifest in all occurrences, apports or disapports, basically making stuff appear and vanish into thin air. Whatever a poltergeist is, it has to build up the strength to do these things; generally, each stage is more impressive than the last. They must somehow sap the people around them of the energy to do this, but aside from the odd sleepless night and excursion to the brink of insanity, what is the cost for the living? If she remembers correctly, the next stage is communication, but whatever is in Philippa's house is mixing up all the stages willy-nilly. If there's a chance of finding this cleaner, and they remember the previous occupants, then it will be a more reliable source than resorting to interfering with contacting the dead themselves.

He Is Your Brother

He's passed this pub thousands of times but has never been in. The decrepit old people with hacking coughs tend to put him off, who stand outside, smoking rollups, unloading great globules of brown phlegm on the pavement beneath the wheels of their mobility scooters. It's an old man's pub, something he has vowed never to set foot in. But still he's through its flaky doors and into an interior that smells of stale booze, wood rot, and age. There's hardly anyone in there, an old man wearing a red fleece with a wolf motif sits at the bar nursing a pint of whatever, faded bird tattoos on his hands. A wrinkled cadaver of a barmaid slumps on a chair behind the bar, doing a crossword from a book. Her hair is a mass of tight, grey curls, her face pinched and unwelcoming. She looks as though she's been sitting there a hundred years or more. Neither offer a greeting as Ranga makes his way to the bar.

"Pint of lager, please." Ranga feels like a schoolboy next to two such ancient people. When the barmaid moves, he expects to see clouds of disturbed dust, hear her joints pop and crack. She never says a thing until she asks for his money, which she pockets and heads back to her crossword.

"Don't mind our Tina," the old man suddenly grumbles. "Her's a right miserable bitch."

"Fuck you, Arthur," the barmaid mutters, without making eye contact.

Ranga nods and reaches for his beer.

"I've got lung cancer," the old man tells him, and for a second he's lost for words.

How the hell do I respond to that? He doesn't care but he forces what he hopes is an expression of concern. "Shit."
"Arr, it is, reckon I've got about two months at the most." The old man sips his drink.
Fucking hell. Ranga wants the rotting floorboards to give way and devour him. "Shit."
"You a fucking parrot?" Arthur says, slamming his glass down.
"Chill out, man, what the hell is wrong with you?"
"I've already told you. I've got lung cancer. Lung cancer. Are you fucking thick, son?" Spit flies from between greenish-grey dentures.
"Calm down, Arthur," the barmaid says, pen thrust out like a magic wand. "Don't start on the lad or you'll spend the last two months of your life going to the fucking off licence."
The old man crumples and begins to cry into his beer.
"I'm sorry son. I've got lung cancer."
"It's okay," Ranga says, feeling suicidal. He reaches out to pat the fella on the shoulder but has second thoughts and quickly finds a dark corner to hide in.

Jesus Christ, this has to be the most depressing pub in the world. Ranga sips at his beer and it tastes like shit. He hears the door creak and wonders what new and wonderfully exotic customer this shit hole has attracted. A heavily pregnant girl pushes someone in a wheelchair, panic flaring up inside him when he immediately recognises the pair.

Keisha has piled on the weight and has lost the fresh youthfulness she once had. Her belly is extended and obscene, almost balancing on the back of the wheelchair.

Noggin is a shapeless blob; the only parts of him that move are his eyes. Whilst Keisha's at the bar, Ranga swiftly heads towards the door. He hears them exchange a greeting.

"Alright, Teen." Keisha.

"'ello bab." Tina the barmaid.

"I've got lung cancer." Name that tune in one.

"I know, mate, I know," Keisha says sympathetically. Just before he pushes through the door, he hears a zombified slur which he presumes is coming from Noggin. Ranga spews an uncontrolled spray of vomit as soon as the fresh air hits him.

As he runs from the pub and the horrors within, they are in pursuit and strobe within his head. A kaleidoscope more colourful than the gruel he's just splattered over the mobility scooter. Images of Noggin ricochet around, pleading for Ranga to leave the pair of them be. His head striking the chest of drawers. The paraplegic hulk that now slumps in the wheelchair.

Ranga grits his teeth and refuses the tears; he will not cry, will not. Two lads come out of one of the trendier bars hand in hand and he immediately swerves out of their way as though they're contagious.

"Fuck's his problem?" one says to the other and Ranga almost wants to thank them for what they've done. All of it comes out, everything, a tsunami of rage and loss but predominantly fear. He throws himself at the pair, mashing the heel of a palm against the closest one's nose and flooring him in an instant. Before the other even has a chance to acknowledge what's happening, Ranga grabs him around the throat and thrusts him against the nearest wall. The lad's hands flail uselessly as Ranga drives a fist into his face. With each punch, he sees Noggin's head striking the chest of drawers, Noggin in the wheelchair, Keisha's ripe belly. The lad keeps on taking the punches until something hard smashes Ranga over the head and he feels himself crumple to the pavement. The lad he'd floored is standing over him with a bottle neck in his hand, nose running with blood. "Do it," Ranga seethes, "do it!"

The boy looks down at the broken bottle in shock. He shrieks and throws it as far as he can before taking his lover in hand and running like hell.

A voice way off says, "I've got lung cancer." Ranga screams into the gutter, beating his fists against the tarmac, and he wishes he had the courage to find that broken bottle and stick it in his own neck. The old man in his head whispers:

Wait.

That's Me

Philippa isn't surprised to discover the mobile number on the cleaner's card is now defunct. She switches on her laptop and runs a search on the name and a whole menagerie of Emilia Szymoniks crop up all around the world but there's no way of knowing which is the one she's looking for. She narrows down the search to people in the area and it comes up with nothing. Even typing in Sparkle Cleaning comes up with a plethora of companies, specialist oven cleaners, window cleaners, even private dentistry. Frustrated, she snatches up the two halves of the card, but when she crumples them, she sees the faintest of digits written in pencil on the back. Her pulse quickens when she sees it's a land-line number.
She picks up the phone and dials.
A woman with a slight accent answers, Polish, or Eastern European.
"Hello, this is a long shot, but am I speaking to Emilia Szymonik?" Philippa says through gritted teeth. "I'm sorry I've called at nine o'clock at night, I didn't notice the time."
"Who is this?"
"Sorry, my name's Philippa, I found a really old business card for Sparkle Cleaning—"
"I don't clean no more, too busy."
Philippa's heart jumps when she realises that this is Emilia. "You're Emilia?"
"Yes, but I told you, no more cleaning. I'm sorry."
"Wait! I don't need a cleaner. Did you ever clean for an old couple or a lady on the Birmingham Road?" She can hear the woman breathing down the line and the time it takes for her to answer seems eternal.

"Yes, I think so, a long time ago. Maybe twenty years."
Fuck, that long. "Do you remember much about the people you cleaned for?"
"Was not people, only an old lady, Vera."
Finding out her name makes it more real. "What was she like?"
Silence, the woman is naturally suspicious. "Why you want to know?"
"I think she's haunting me." Philippa can't think of anything else to say, no elaborate on-the-spot fib. This will be the end of the conversation for sure.
Instead of the laughter she's been expecting, she hears a slow intake of breath.
"Where did you find my card? Are you relative?"
"No, I'm no relation. Originally, I found your card down the back of the fireplace."
"What do you mean, originally?"
"It's a long story."
"Would you like me to come around?"
"Oh my god, yeah, that would be fantastic!" Philippa is surprised by the woman's suggestion but pleased that she was the one to make it.
She tries Ryan's number after making arrangements with Emilia the following day but there's no reply. The only friend she knows him to have is Noggin, the one who'd beat the crap out of him six months before.
There is no point in worrying, it is beyond her control. Although she knows she would find it hard to sleep without him by her side after the incident with Layla and the TV, she has no other choice.

Layla gets shut in the kitchen despite her protests, but Philippa can't trust her after what she did earlier, not yet. She reluctantly crawls into bed and is curious to find it's Niamh that she wishes were here rather than her fiancé. She falls asleep listening to Layla pining and scratching at the kitchen door.

She doesn't know how long she's been asleep but when she wakes up she can't move. Strong, rough-skinned hands pin her down at the arms, drag her from slumber. She opens her eyes and sees the old man leering down at her, hair straggled and straw-like, face haggard, and hanging with jowls of fat. The stench of him is overpowering; sweat and tobacco. He fades out into nothing, just below the collarbones. She screams and hears the dog throw itself against the door.
Footsteps race up through the house, fists pound against the bedroom door, and even though she can still feel the places where he restrained her, the man is gone.
Ryan bursts into the room wearing boxer shorts and a startled expression. She doesn't question his return, and runs into his arms. "He was here, he was here. He was here!"

Lay All Your Love on Me

He doesn't know what the fuck she's going on about. She's hysterical. There's no way there's anyone in the room with them now. He's had enough of this bat-shit craziness. The dog is going nuts in the kitchen.

"It's okay, it's okay."

"He was here, he had me on the bed."

"Phil, there's no one here. I've been here since god knows when."

"He disappeared," she says, becoming more animated. "It was the old man that used to live here."

He rolls his eyes without being able to stop himself.

"You know what? I don't care if you believe me or not, I'm doing something about this."

"I never said I didn't believe you."

"You didn't have to."

His mother used to believe in all kinds of shit like this but she also believed in going to church at Easter and Christmas. It didn't make her right. Niamh has been putting weird witchy shit in her head. "I believe what I can see with my own eyes, Phil."

"What about the television?"

"You can't keep saying 'the ghosts did it' every time stuff happens."

She looks at him in disbelief. "You're honestly saying you've not detected anything weird in this house? No strange smells, anything?"

"Okay, maybe once or twice I've come in and it smells like you've had a cheeky fag or had someone round you ain't been telling me about, but—"

"That's him! That's the old man. The place always feels depressing, colder, and there's a horrible smell of B.O and pipe smoke."

He can see she genuinely believes this shit, which furthers his theory that she's crazy. "Look, we're going to have to agree to disagree on this, unless," he says, throwing his hands up, "what's-his-face decides to put on some theatrics for yours truly."

Philippa nods but he knows she isn't happy.

"Look, I've got to go to the agency about another job. Are you going to be okay?"

"No, don't leave me, please."

She's clearly rattled but she'll be even more pissed if he doesn't go and get something sorted so he can get some more money this month. "Babe, I've got to."

"He tried to rape me just like he did Niamh."

That fucking witch. That's where all this is coming from.

"Is there someone who can come round?"

Her eyes light up. "Emilia!"

"Who's Emilia?"

"She's coming round at half nine. She used to work here."

"What do you mean she used to work here?"

"She was the cleaner for Vera. That's the old lady who lived here before, the one who likes ABBA."

"Fucking hell," he says, trying not to let his amusement show, "you're cray-cray."

"Fuck off."

"Look, I'll be back as soon as possible," he says, and quickly heads towards the door. "Don't let that Emma, or whatever she's called, put any ideas in your head, Niamh does more than enough of that."

Elaine

She wishes Niamh was with her but she has work. She keeps herself busy by tidying and rearranging things that do not need tidied or rearranged. The knock at the door makes her jump an inch off the floor and yet she rushes to it, desperate to see the person on the other side. Emilia is a short skinny woman with shoulder-length blonde hair, expertly applied makeup, and she looks and smells exquisite. Philippa invites her in. They go into the kitchen whilst Layla introduces herself and Philippa prepares drinks.

Once seated in the lounge she sees Emilia look around the room, her eyes staying on the broken television for a second too long.

"That happened last night."

Emilia nods.

"There haven't been that many incidents of things moving by themselves but that was one of them."

"Okay."

Philippa can tell Emilia doesn't believe her and she totally gets that, she wouldn't believe her either.

"The place looks very different to when Vera was here," Emilia says, breaking the awkward silence. "So much more space."

"Oh, was she a hoarder, then?"

Emilia shakes her head and smiles. "No, she just collected a lot of different things."

"Can you tell me about her?"

Emilia puts her mug on the coffee table. "Now, I don't mean to be rude, but I don't believe in all this mumbo-jumbo."

"Oh God, I didn't until I came here, and my best friend says she sees spirits all the time."

"Very well. Why don't you tell me what has been happening, and if any of it sounds like the Vera I once cleaned for, I'll let you know."

"Okay." Philippa thinks back to moving-in day and when she noticed the strangeness about the place. "It's mostly the atmosphere of the house. When I first moved in it felt wonderful, like I was a little kid again, as though there was something unseen watching out for me. I felt at home."

"Aren't these normal feelings for someone when they move into new place?"

Philippa nods. "Yeah, I guess so, but there are other things too. My phone kept playing ABBA music and whenever the house felt happy it smelled different, of oranges and —"

"Citronella," Emilia whispers.

"What's that?"

"She, Vera, used to have citronella diffusers and flavoured incense all over the place. It's an oil, smells a little like citrus fruits and grass, it's a great natural insect repellent."

Philippa remembers the mystery insect stings. "Did she always have a problem with bugs?"

Emilia laughs dryly. "Yeah, you could say that." She looks above Philippa's head. "Did your estate agent or landlord tell you about the ceiling in here being replaced?"

"Oh yeah, the wasps nest?"

"*Just* about the wasp nest?"

"What do you mean?"

"It was before I came to work here but we would talk, she got lonely."

"What happened?"

"I don't know exactly what happened but there was an intruder, someone who knew them. Vera was living with her mother and husband then. The man, he hid in the attic."

"Oh my god."

"Vera had complained about a humming in the roof. The intruder disturbed a massive wasps' nest and came through the ceiling."

"Jesus!"

"That's not the worst, he accidentally killed Vera's mother. Landed on her when he fell."

Holy holy holy fuck, how many people have died in this place?

"What you say, the happiness, citrus, and especially ABBA, sounds like Vera very much. She was a lovely woman. Young at heart."

All Philippa can do is smile.

"I don't know what happens," Emilia says, "when we go, when we die, but it would be nice to think we leave something behind aside from the memories, for those that still remember us."

"Was she happy here?"

"Oh, of course." Emilia virtually beams. "She grew up in this house. It was her parents'." Then her face darkens. "But she had many, many, bad years here too."

"Her husband."

Emilia looks shocked. "How did you know?"

Philippa takes a deep breath before slowly releasing it. "He's here too."

Bang-A-Boomerang

He feels like utter shite. There's nothing worse than spending half the night in the fucking gutter—other than spending half the night in the fucking gutter stone cold sober. He knows he's royally fucked in the head; the voice of who he assumes is his dad and the complete breakdown he had after visiting the most depressing pub in the world assure him of that fact. Tina, Lung Cancer, Keisha and Noggin. It's been a long, long time since he's wanted to kill himself but last night he was as close as he'd ever been. He has nothing. Is nothing. He wishes he'd never become involved with Philippa. He'd given up everything to be with that doolally bint because it seemed better than his previous situation, but now he would give anything for it to be the way it was. He and Noggin doing what they wanted, when they wanted.

An older side of him, one that rarely emerges, tells him he can make the best of this situation, turn it all around, that he can't keep acting the cunt now he's in his forties, but the bigger, more selfish side wants things his way.

He's late for the employment agency; Jesus, he'd only got about half an hour's sleep on the sofa before that dotty bitch started screaming she was being raped by fucking Casper. He stinks, he knows he stinks, and the smarmy expression on the agent's face makes him want to stave it in with the humorous coffee mug that sits on the desk in his cubicle.

"You're twenty minutes late. You know there are plenty of people who want to work—"

Ranga can't. He just can't. The bloke is like twelve years old, has something on his top lip that looks like shedded cat fur, and is so smug that it radiates from him.

He doesn't even know he's done it until the monitor crashes to the floor and the kid is recoiling, eyes agog. A klaxon sounds, an under-the-desk alarm, and the agent looks in fear for his life.

Ranga laughs, although it's more bark than laugh, turns heel, and heads towards the exit.

Well, that's gone and fucked that.

It feels like relief when he walks away from the building. He's on a mission of self-destruction that will end with either death or incarceration.

Voulez-Vous

Emilia appears genuinely saddened by what Philippa has said; her mouth opens and closes but nothing comes out.
"Did she say much about him?"
"No, not really, only that he was an abusive, racist bastard."
"I guess a lot of her generation were."
"No, Vera wasn't. She had such a lust for life. She collected things from all around the world which she found in charity shops, other people's unwanted holiday souvenirs."
Philippa's heart breaks a little.
"She never got the chance to travel. Roger, her husband, wouldn't allow it, they were lucky to get away to the seaside."
Philippa notices tears in Emilia's eyes.
"Just before she died, we talked about going on a tour of Poland, my country. I was a student then, living with my parents, but I had savings; I wanted to help grant this wonderful woman her wish to leave this soil for the first time in her life." She dabs at her eyes with her sleeves.
"We were actually going to do it. She went to fetch the passport papers the morning she died." Her eyes are red from rubbing. "I was the last person she spoke to."
Philippa reaches forward and takes her hands. "What happened?"
"Heart attack. We were going through a heatwave and she told me she was already feeling under the weather but she went out, into town, as it was her appointed day to do so. There was an incident in town, an altercation, which I think played a part in upsetting her further."
"What?"

"A teenage layabout pickpocketed her and she confronted him about it. It shook her up." Emilia gazes at a space near the window; she doesn't bother to stop the tears now. "That's where she used to sit. She loved looking out of the window."

"Fucking bastard. Sorry. Was anything done about the mugger?"

"No, you are right. No need for apologies. He was a fucking bastard, acted the young gentleman, told her about his tattoo meaning fearless in Japanese or something, helped her onto the bus and stole her purse."

"The piece of shit."

Emilia nods in agreement. "So what are you going to do about your problems?"

"I have no idea. I have a friend, like I might have said, who knows about this kind of thing, so I guess I'll leave it up to her."

"Okay, well keep in tou—"

The citronella hits them both like tear gas, it's overwhelming. Emilia jumps to her feet, eyes and mouth wide. She's breathless, as if she's having an asthma attack. "Emilia."

They both hear the woman's voice. It's coming from far away, above them in a back bedroom, and sounds distant, as if they were in a mansion and not a bungalow.

Emilia crushes her fingers in her hand almost to the point where it hurts; the tears are pouring down her face but her grin reaches her eyes.

"That's the first time she's spoken," Philippa whispers, as they bask in the warmth of Vera's loving embrace like two long-lost daughters. It's magical, a spectral mother's love so strong it feels as though the soles of their feet are inches from the floor. A holy rapture.

Then an almighty crash resounds throughout the place as the front door slams open and Ryan bursts in screaming, "The fucking backstabbing cunts!"

Intermezzo No. 1

Rosemary
Mugwort
Juniper
Sage
Himalayan salt lamp

Niamh repeats the shopping list in her head. A mantra
not unlike Dorothy's lions and tigers and bears. Oh my.
Thank God for Holland and Barratt. The one-stop shop
for all modern-day witches. The Himalayan salt lamp she
buys from Amazon. She loads tiny vials of essential oils,
all labelled in her own teeny handwriting, into a small
leather satchel along with incense sticks made from cedar
and Palo Santo wood, a handful of mixed rock crystals,
table salt, and a pair of silver Baoding balls. She secretly
calls it her witch-kit.

All day at work she's had a feeling in the pit of her
stomach that things are coming to a head with Philippa
and her haunted house, and trusting her intuition has
been the only way she's made it so far in life. There will
be no contact, no séances, just a strict, ruthless, ritualistic
cleansing of all bad energy.

Hey, Hey Helen

Layla whimpers and hides as soon as Ranga barges in the room. Philippa and some older, blonde tart stare at him holding each other's hands like a pair of fucking carpet-munchers. He feels the greasy leer slide up his face. Is that what's going on? *Room for another one*? "Aye, aye, what are you pair up to?"

The woman lets go of Philippa's hand and averts her eyes.

"Ey, don't stop on my account," he says, slumping on to the settee and clomping his feet on the coffee table.

Philippa turns toward him excitedly. "The lady who lived here spoke to us!"

The blonde nods and the two women grin at one another, two schoolgirls with a secret.

"Course she fucking did. Tell you to hold each other's hands and get it on, did she? Likes watching girl on girl, does she? Dirty old mare."

"Why are you being so bloody obscene?" Philippa snaps at him. The other woman looks uncomfortable as fuck.

"I'm not the one who's been caught hand in hand with a complete stranger!" he bites back, waving a hand at the evidence in front of him.

He remembers now. Philippa had mentioned that some bird who used to clean the house was coming around to talk about the old biddy that used to live here. Emily or something. She looks at him with wild eyes, her nostrils flared in defiance as if she's about to start having a go. He locks eyes on her and mentally dares her.

"You're an idiot," Philippa states.

Ranga shrugs. "I'm not the one believing in fucking ghosts."

"Philippa, I should go," the woman says, and he notices her accent and sniggers.

"Yis," he says, mimicking her accent badly, "mebbe I should go too."

If looks could kill, the woman's glare would have caused him to combust.

"You're a fucking pig!" Philippa shouts and strikes out with her foot as she leads the woman towards the front door.

Knowing Me, Knowing You

His laughter comes from the living room as they walk outside.

"I'm so sorry, he's not well," Philippa begins, but stops mid-sentence when Emilia grabs her wrist, her face whitewashed.

"What does that symbol on his arm mean?"

"Huh?"

"His tattoo!" Her fingers dig into the skin.

Philippa's breath catches in her throat as she remembers the day of their first proper date. In the park, when she'd met Layla. The dog bounding over after playing in the park, leaping up to slobber all over her face when they'd moved in for a kiss. Him physically scolding the animal and then apologising when she told him off for it.

"She's just a bit reckless. Fearless, like me." He'd revealed the tattoo on his arm.

It's got to be a coincidence. Please let it be a coincidence.

She can tell Emilia knows she's put two and two together. The woman grips her hand in both of hers. "Maybe this is why the bad things are happening. Maybe Vera doesn't want him in her house."

"Oh God," Philippa moans, feeling the building hulk behind her, the shadow it casts malevolent and cold. She feels like the copper in that weird seventies film Niamh made her watch as a kid, The Wicker Man, when he sees what the audience had been waiting for. The spoiler is in the title. "Oh, Jesus Christ, no."

She re-enters the house as though it really is something from a horror story. Her hands shake as she reaches for the door handle, her instincts telling her to run, rabbit, run, run, run. He's there in the lounge and it's full of the smell of the *other* him. Vera's husband, Ryan, they're both the same. He's sprawled across the settee, one hand stuffed down the front of his tracksuit bottoms scratching himself, the other behind his head. She sees the tattoo, it's all she can see. She confronts him whilst she still has her back to the exit.

"You did it. You killed her."

His bemused expression turns to a mixture of confusion and anger. "The fuck you on about? I ain't killed anyone." Philippa detects something else in his eyes, though, fear. He's *not* fearless. Genuinely fearless people don't need a tattoo in Japanese to announce the fact. "You stole her purse and the shock of it gave her a heart attack."

Hollow laughter escapes him. "What the fuck you on? Is that what your Russian girlfriend said? Don't tell me, she's one of them fucking psychos like Witch-Tits?"

"Don't speak about my friend like that. She's always there for me."

"Yeah, I bet she is," he says with a lecherous slur, "wouldn't surprise me if she was a dyke like your other girlfriend."

He's avoiding answering. Changing the subject. "Did you mug Vera?"

He sits up fast and takes pleasure when she flinches. "I'm not listening to this shit anymore. This is my house too!" Philippa gasps. "This is not your house. And it never will be!"

The smell of old man swamps them. Ryan moves with the speed of a cat, clamps a hand around her throat, and slams her against the door, closing it. "We'll fucking well see about that, you ungrateful little cunt." His other hand thrusts between her legs and she immediately brings her knee up as hard as she can towards his testicles. He recoils, bent double, hissing obscenities as Roger's smell surrounds her and chokes her almost as much as Ryan's hand. She pulls at the door, gets it open an inch, but an unseen force slams it shut again. Layla, the other frightened and abused female in Ryan's life, screams from the kitchen. Philippa looks at the dog sorrowfully, Ryan reaches out for her. Using all of her strength, fear, and anger, she pulls the door open and runs out of the house.

Ode to Freedom

Ice baths and meditation have been keeping Niamh's demons away. Especially since her suicide attempt. Failing that, getting absolutely pissed or stoned helps. She's sitting cross-legged on her favourite spot, beneath the silver birch. A slight breeze ruffles her curls, there's sunlight on her upturned soles, and the sound of lawnmowers and far-off schoolchildren playing. It's pure and beautiful and she won't let anything penetrate her bubble. The two men who pass her shouting, "Alright darlin', nice day for it," are registered, but only on the cusp of her consciousness. There are limits to how much outside solitude you can get on a stretch of grass and trees nestled between six tower blocks, but she makes the best of what she's got. An airplane flies overhead, its vapour trail drawing across the blue. In her head she's up there on a cloud with only the birds for company. Happy thoughts of her childhood, when she was really young, when she was a little...different, play for her. How she used to think that birds slept in the clouds, making nests on huge downy sky pillows. She would imagine growing wings and flying up there to be with them, to listen to their strange high-pitched snores. She pictures that now, she's not on the grass in the middle of a council estate, she's three miles up, in the clouds away from anyone else, soaring above the busy world, burning her skin in the sun.

"Neeeeeeeeem!"

The sound of her friend in distress jolts her back to the earth with crashing reality. Philippa runs across the grass towards her, red-faced. But she's definitely not wearing running clothes.

Ryan is close behind.

Niamh is on her feet in seconds; she runs barefoot across the grass and grabs Philippa's hands. "What the fuck is going on?"
"He killed her. He killed Vera!" Philippa shrieks the sentence out; Niamh has never seen her so distraught.
Ryan crosses over the road, narrowly avoiding being hit by the Ring and Ride minibus.
Niamh doesn't know who the hell Philippa is talking about but the mere fact that she's petrified and running from someone she's labelled a killer is enough. There's no time to run, so she plants herself in front of Philippa just as Ryan steps on to the grass.
"Get out of the way," Ryan spits, towering over her, "this is between me and her."
"I don't know what the fuck you've done but she doesn't want you anywhere near her so fuck off." Niamh seethes, she's light on her feet, refusing to let him get past her.
Philippa is a wreck behind her, she hasn't seen him as bad as this for years. This man has slowly rubbed away her hard veneer and found the wood beneath soft and rotten. Has made the years Niamh has spent helping her friend, her love, build up her defence mechanism against anxiety, depression, and body confidence obsolete.
"Leave her alone!" Niamh hisses with more venom than she's ever given in her life.

Unsurprisingly, the man who's a good foot taller than her laughs in her face. His attention turns to her; she feels his eyes roam up and down, up and down, lingering on the exposed flesh that her vest and shorts fail to cover. "What the fuck are you going to do about it? Eh?" His head juts forward like a chicken's and once again he laughs when she flinches. "Get out of my way or I'll fucking split you in two, you mad hippy bitch. It's your fault she's off her fucking trolley."

His hand darts out.

Dance (While the Music Still Goes On)

Ryan's monstrous, like the chavvy offspring of Slenderman and the Grinch. His hand reaches out towards Niamh's breast and it's what she's been waiting for. Niamh has him face-down on the grass in seconds, his arm bent at an awkward, uncomfortable angle behind his back. She presses her knee down in the middle of his spine and twists his arm harder.

"Get off me," Ryan screams, in genuine pain.

"I should fucking snap it, you abusive cunt." Niamh is truly beautiful in that moment, a fucking warrior princess. Philippa loves her so much.

"You wouldn't believe the amount of shit I've taken from people like you."

Philippa has lost count of the number of martial arts Niamh has practised since primary school but she has never seen her put any of them to use until now.

"I'm not going anywhere," Ryan forces out, "until she tells me herself."

Philippa moves around and crouches close, but not too close. "I don't want to see you any more, Ryan. Your stuff, what little of it there is, will be outside the house by nine o'clock tonight."

The commotion has attracted other people milling about on the estate; the two men who passed Niamh moments before cross back over the grounds towards them.

"Bitch," he roars at her and squeals when Niamh twists his arm further. He grits his teeth against the pain and shouts, "Fuck you, you fucking who—"

Niamh twists harder so he can't even talk. "Now, I'm going to let you go, and if you try anything, I will really fucking hurt you. This is nothing compared to what I can do."

Money, Money, Money

The fucking crafty little bitch, Ranga thinks, bending his forearm back and forth trying to alleviate the pain in his elbow and shoulder. *Bitch nearly broke my fucking arm.* He tells himself that he would have got her off, that he really enjoyed the feel of her bare thighs pinning him against the grass, but it's hard to believe when his arm hurts so much. If it hadn't had been for the pair of men coming to their rescue he would have. He would have seen to both of them. He needs something to take the edge off his anger before he does something stupid to himself that will leave him unable to exact his revenge.

Fists clenched, he steams through town, ready to confront anyone who so much as sniffs in his direction.

He doesn't even know what Philippa was on about. Sure, he's snatched loads of purses in his time. Speaking of which, he spots a middle-aged man pulling notes out of a cash machine ahead of him and stuffing them into his wallet. He follows him to see where he's going, taking note of exactly which pocket he stowed his wallet in. But he's never killed any old ladies, though, he'd remember that. She's let some nutter witch bitch and some Polish tart get into her fucking head and fill it with bullshit. The man jogs up the steps of the bus station and nips into the toilets, which are nestled between a pair of empty shop outlets. Ranga isn't far behind him.

The man is standing in front of one of the urinals, resting a hand on the wall. A quick inspection tells Ranga that just one of the stalls is occupied. Wasting absolutely no time he launches himself across the pissy floor and barges his shoulder into the man's back. The man's face smacks against the wall when they crash against the urinal.
Ranga grabs his head and smashes it again against the wall. Before the man can even register what's happening, Ranga's hand is pulling the wallet from his pocket. The man lashes back with an elbow but misses. Ranga makes to run but the man, still dazed by the head trauma, grabs on to him. He's a lot younger than Ranga first thought, and he's genuinely surprised when the man pulls a knife on him. "Give me back my wallet," he screams, and slashes the knife through the air between them.
Ranga feels the blade slide down his arm a second before the pain sinks in.
The man — on closer inspection, he's more of a teenager — looks petrified.
Ranga takes advantage of his guilt and makes a grab for his knife-hand.
They struggle; the kid is no match for someone twice his age, someone who's been on the streets doing this shit longer than he's been alive. He's more worried about getting Ranga's blood on him, probably thinks it's infected.
The rage and the humiliation rocket through Ranga's system, coursing through his veins like heroin, and the youth takes the brunt of his fury head-on. The knife-hand is twisted, a lesser-skilled variation on the move that Niamh played on him, and the knife is turned and pushed up and into the boy's abdomen.

His face pales; Ranga sees in the mirrors that his face matches the boy's, and he shoves a bloody hand over the boy's mouth to keep him from screaming. The lad falls back, arse in the urinal, and Ranga grips the hand still holding the knife tighter as its hold loosens. The fear sets in fast and Ranga pushes and pulls the kid's knife-hand back and forth, back and forth, back and forth, until he's still. Ranga springs back, one eye on the dripping dead boy sat in the urinal, the other on the closed stall door. His arm pisses blood onto the tiles. The toilet in the cubicle is flushed and he has seconds to get out of this hole he's dug himself in. His t-shirt is covered in blood — mostly the kid's, he reckons — so he yanks it off and wraps it around his forearm as he runs.

As soon as he leaves the toilets, he lowers his face and walks at a normal pace. No one bats an eyelid at a skinny middle-aged chav with his top off on a sunny day.

When he's at a safe enough distance he goes through the wallet but makes sure not to put it in any bins just yet. You can't trash the wallet in the town centre nowadays, there's CCTV everywhere and once that kid is found, all hell will break loose. He counts the notes inside. Forty quid in ten-pound notes. It'll do.

The Way Old Friends Do

"I can't believe you did that," Philippa says, after Ryan's run off.

Niamh smiles, lets the two men who'd come back to investigate think they'd rescued them from the nasty man. "I just feel like I need to have a shower after getting so physical with him."

"You can have one at mine."

"Err, no, thank you," Niamh says, incredulously.

"Shit, yeah, to be honest with you I'm kind of scared about even getting undressed there now. I saw him the other morning."

Niamh freezes. "The old man?"

"Yeah, I woke up." Philippa shudders at the memory. "I could feel someone on top of me. He faded out below the shoulders."

"Why the fuck didn't you tell me?"

"So much happened at once. I fought with Ryan because I wanted him to stay, and then Emilia came around, which I had totally forgotten about."

"Who the fuck is Emilia? The cleaner?"

Philippa groans at her friend's forgetfulness. "She's the reason I came running here. She said Vera, the lady who used to live in my house, was mugged the day she died."

"Oh my god, and you reckon it was Ry—"

"She said the mugger had a tattoo on his forearm. Japanese symbol meaning fearless. It's what he has on his arm, Neem."

"Shit."

"Yeah, I'm sure it was him. He has a very chequered past."

"Fuck."

For a moment they stand staring down the hill in the direction Ryan ran off in, catching their breath, getting over the shock of it all.

Niamh breaks the quiet with her relentless optimism. "We'll go up to mine, get my witch-kit, and then go and zap the bad shit from your house."
"Whatever you say."
They head inside one of the tower blocks and wait for the lift.
"I reckon he was feeding off of him."
"Ryan?"
"Yeah, think about it. The time I heard the male voice, and, to put it lightly, felt his presence, was after you had a row when he turned up unannounced." Niamh jabs her finger accusatively at a floor number.
"We did not have a row."
"Well, whatever it was. You were pissed off that he invaded our girl-time and the old prick floating around your house fed off the negative vibes."
It makes sense. Philippa knows things escalated when he turned up and they got together.
They go in Niamh's flat, it's the first time Philippa has been in this one. The first thing she notices, after how spotlessly clean everything is, is the spectacular view from the windows overlooking the town. "You're so high up."
Niamh smiles. "Yep. I love it up here in my cloud. It's like being in heaven." She pulls a face. "Well, if you can ignore the neighbours."
"Everyone has a stereotypical image of tower blocks: broken lifts, pissy floors, graffiti."

"Yeah, this one's alright, for now, but it's mostly old folk still, who were here when they were built in the seventies. You should see some of the other blocks where the original tenants have moved on. Right, I'm going for a shower, I won't be long. Stop looking all awkward and clumsy and make yourself at home. I'm sure you can find stuff."

"Yes, Mum." Philippa takes in the surroundings whilst Niamh readies herself. She loves all the hippy stuff Niamh has all over the place: posters about Buddhism, little statues of various deities, compartments for candles and incense.

The living room is an abundance of green, there are plants everywhere and she's not at all surprised to see Niamh hasn't got a television. Where one would set the TV is a gigantic photo collage spanning the entire wall. There are photos of nights out, holidays, random objects, and people she thought she had forgotten. There are photos of them when they were children and very, very different. There are flyers from restaurants, nightclubs, little plastic shopping bags of stores long closed, neatly folded to display their logo. Little trinkets tacked to the wall, pieces of string, festival bands, bottle tops, a pen. There's even one or two pages torn from paperbacks with passages highlighted in various colours. Philippa heard Niamh mention her Memory Wall, remembered a previous incarnation of it in her bedroom when they were kids, but is amazed by how it's matured.

"All done."

Niamh startles her. "Fucking hell, that was quick!" she says, taking in the sight of Niamh wrapped in a pair of towels.

"Not really, I've been at least ten minutes."

Phillipa laughs, not sure if this is an exaggeration or not. She cocks a thumb at her wall. "One could get lost for days looking at this. It's amazing."

Niamh grins. "One day, I want a house, and I'll cover a whole room with photos like this."

"That would be amazing! You could even put bigger ones, in case of failing eyesight, on the ceiling."

"Yass, girl!" Niamh says, holding her hand up for a high-five and looking at her ceiling excitedly, imagining the possibility.

"It's a lovely place. You always make the best of everything."

"Wasn't when I moved in. Had right bad energy. I had to cleanse the place three times."

"Oh," Philippa says, feeling awkward, still skeptical even after everything. "Well, it worked, I presume?"

Niamh bounces on her feet. "Deffo. I've not failed a cleansing yet. It's all about willpower and what you've got in your witch bag."

"Well, I hope you've got the good shit in there today."

The sun burns their skin as they leave the tower block; it doesn't feel like the right sort of weather for chasing away ghosts.

It's beach weather, beer garden weather.

A queasy feeling stirs Philippa's guts, one she's always likened to a cold octopus sloshing around inside her, when she remembers the last time they'd sat in a beer garden in weather like this.

When that bag of crap came sailing over the fence and the glass shattered and cut up poor Katherine's face. And then her downward spiral into suicide.

So much shit had happened since, and the house had felt amazing.

It still does, on and off.
Why had the bad woken up?
What had triggered it?
Did anything trigger it, or were Vera and Roger waiting for the right vessels to give them the energy they needed? Could Niamh rid the place of both of them or only the negative energy? Surely they would want to move on. What was this, a husband-and-wife feud that continued beyond the fucking grave?

The people in the town centre are sluggish with the heat. A woman, hugely pregnant, grunts with the effort of pushing a wheelchair that's laden with shopping bags on each handle. Even the person in the chair holds a bag. There's something about the girl that seems familiar but Philippa can't place her. As she and Niamh flit across the street to go around them, she half-turns and glimpses the couple's faces. Keisha Williams. Freya's little sister. The barmaid. Philippa sees the struggle on her face, the sweat and the frustration, her extended belly, and can't help but pity her. She's done too much too young.
"No fucking way!" Philippa stops.
Without saying anything to Niamh, without having said a single sentence to him whilst he helped Ryan decorate her house, she shouts. "Noggin!"
The couple stop and Keisha's immediate reaction is fear. Philippa sees the man is able to move his head and one arm. His expression is indifferent.
"Who are they?" Niamh whispers as they cross back over the road.
"Hello Keisha," is all Philippa says, and the young girl's face is overcome with a guilt she can't disguise.
"Congratulations." Philippa eyes her belly with fake excitement.

There's a flicker of fire behind the girl's eyes. "Come to gloat, have you?"

"What about?"

Keisha avoids the question. "I take it you're not with Ranga anymore, then?"

Philippa grimaces at his horrible nickname, she tries to speak but the words won't come out. She shakes her head. "How did you find out?" Keisha says, lowering her eyes and picking at the wheelchair handles.

"I don't quite know what you're on about, Keisha."

Keisha studies the back of Noggin's head.

"What happened to you?" Philippa asks him and he says something back that she can't understand. There's a scar on his head, he's been in an accident, had a tumour, or maybe a stroke or something, he can't talk properly at all. How the hell could he have beaten the crap out of Ryan? Even the few times she'd seen them together, he was the one who'd acted like Ryan's sidekick, his stooge, not the other way around. "Fuck it," she says dryly, as the cogs in her brain start adding more and more things together. She feels Niamh's hand on her arm.

It hurts like fuck to say it but she has to force the words out of her mouth. Her arm is heavy when she lifts it to point at Noggin. "Ryan did this, didn't he?"

Keisha nods and lays a hand on her swollen stomach. "And this."

Philippa's legs give way. The pavement burns, but not half as much as Keisha's revelations.

Soldiers

There are no friends left, only people he knows, people he owes. Ranga hasn't seen G for at least a year, and hopes to Christ himself that he's not been banged up — or worse. He repeatedly presses numbers four and five and buzzes G's flat. This block is on the shitty side of town, there's crap everywhere outside, as if people have thrown their rubbish off balconies and out of windows. The car park, bereft of any vehicles, is littered with broken glass and nappy explosions. They were supposed to be condemning the bloody place, especially after Grenfell, but it was still home to some.

The blood had soaked through the shirt and he needed something else to wrap it in; if G had anything else it would be an added bonus.

"Yeah," comes a tinny voice from the intercom.

"G-Man, it's Ranga, let me in, please."

There's no welcoming reply, only the high-pitched beep of the door unlocking.

The foyer is a junk room: broken tables and chairs and a filthy sofa that reeks of shit and piss. *Jesus fucking Christ.* Ranga knows that this is what he's got to look forward to now, he'll end up here or somewhere worse, if such a place exists. Unsurprisingly, the lifts don't work, so he makes the trek of climbing up eight flights of stairs.

G's waiting on the landing, all three hundred pounds of him, a sweatshirt hood almost obscuring his black eyes.

Behind him, a door is open, releasing a toxic miasma of marijuana and cat piss. The flat next door to his is boarded up and covered with graffiti tags. He takes one look at Ranga's arm, scratches his bushy black beard, and nods at the open door.

G's place is just as rank as the rest of the block. Scabby-eyed cats, Ranga spots at least half a dozen, roam all over every surface, one is curled up inside a colossal pair of stained pants.

"What do you need?"

"Something for my arm and something for the pain."

G nods. "How much you got?"

Ranga takes out the stolen wallet. "Twenty quid."

G sees the identity card inside. "Going to cost you a lot more than that."

Ranga closes his eyes and contemplates turning around and running, knowing that once he lets G help him it will be a different sort of running he'll be doing. He'll be in debt with him for years.

He has no choice; there is nowhere else, no one else. He forces a smile. "I am at your service."

G's laughter is deep and throaty, God-like.

So Long

"So how the hell do we cleanse the house?" Philippa asks Niamh. They're in the living room watching their reflections in the cracked telly. Layla bounces between them, over the moon to have company.

"I'll get everything ready then you can help me, just do what you've got to do."

"It'll take me five minutes to bag up all his shit," Philippa says, breaking a black bag off a roll.

They set off in separate directions, Philippa loading anything of Ryan's into the bin liner whilst Niamh whizzes around, Layla in tow, opening all the windows.

"This isn't just because it's burning in here," Niamh explains, "we've got to let all the bad juju out."

"So, ghosts can walk through walls but not through glass?"

Niamh laughs. "Yeah, man, they totally bump into it like this." She runs across the floor and smacks into an invisible force field, palms flat against thin air.

Philippa grins and cackles as Niamh knocks on the imaginary glass, her left foot tapping in time with her knuckles.

"You're a nutter."

Niamh winks at her and turns to open the living room window and something unseen knocks her on her arse.

"Holy shit," she exclaims, "did you see that?"

Layla's throat thunder starts up.

Philippa rushes to Niamh's aid, knowing she didn't fake that, but she's still laughing. "Oh," she says in a baby voice, "don't the spooky-wookies like having the piss taken out of them?"

Philippa doesn't need to help her stand up, she's back on her feet within seconds.

Niamh spins on the spot. "You know what? I'm not fucking scared of you! Live people are so much worse." She turns to Philippa. "Things might get busy when we do this shit. They might try to put up a fight. Use everything they have left to stop us. It's important that you remain positive, not to get scared, they feed off that shit. Take the piss, make fun. Or at the very least ignore them and carry on as normal. They're nothing more than disembodied bullies."

Philippa takes a deep breath and nods and gets back to packing Ryan's things.

Niamh flits about, placing unusual objects in weird places. Little ramekins with fragrant oils on windowsills and the mantelpiece alongside shards of multicoloured crystals. Candles are set but not yet lit, incense sticks, a big pink crystal lamp. It takes her an age. Philippa carries Ryan's stuff out of the house and sits the bags by the front gate; when she returns, Niamh is pouring table salt around the perimeter of the house in a meticulous, unbroken line.

"Right, everything is ready," Niamh says, when she's thoroughly checked everything is in place.

After all they've done, the sun has set, and Philippa wants it over and done with. "Are we going to start?"

Niamh nods. "I guess so. You've taken the phone off the hook, yeah? We don't want any disturbances."

"Yeah, but what if he comes and gets his stuff in the middle of it?"

"Just ignore him and concentrate on what we're doing, okay? His shit is outside, that's it."

"Okay."

Niamh hands her an oblong parcel, cigarette papers wrapped around something bound with string.

"We gonna get high now?" Philippa says, holding it to her lips.

Niamh grins. "You are a comedic genius, Phil, you know that?"

"Is it a spring roll?"

"Please," Niamh says, holding her stomach, "stop. I can't take it anymore. My sides are literally splitting."

"Sarky bitch."

"Don't you fucking know it. Right, this is a smudging stick."

Philippa giggles. "Sounds a bit rude," she says, adopting a masculine voice, "alright darling, can I show you my smudging stick?"

Niamh's laughter is genuine now. "Seriously, stop. This is filled with my own special recipe. We light these fuckers once I've lit everything else and waft the smoke around making happy noises and filling this place with good vibes."

"Been ages since I had a good vibe. My batteries ran out."

"That's the spirit!" Niamh says, and they both cackle at her accidental pun.

"It will also help if we can think of something to chant in unison."

"Like the twins in The Shining?"

"Exactly, except we don't want these fuckers to stay forever and ever and ever."

"Good point."

"Something along the lines of 'Move on to somewhere new. You are not welcome here.'"

"'This is not your house'?" Philippa suggests, thinking back to the betting slip, the situation, the number of times that phrase has already come up since she moved here. Yes." Niamh gets up and takes a box of matches off the table. "Right, let's do this, babe."

I Have a Dream

His head is a cacophony of coercive cunts. Every little ghost comes back to haunt him. His dad, his dad's friends, Uncle Billy from when he was little, to name but a few. Voices he thought were locked so far away inside, nothing would ever amplify them and cause him to remember. Scenes play with crystal clarity, fucking HD-quality flashbacks of childhood traumas long forgotten. Like when he was six and being chased home by Tony Lyons and Freddie Lucas, both older boys shouting that they were going to pull his trousers down and stick their bicycle pumps up his arsehole and make him fatter like them because he was such a skinny little runt. His father, bearing witness to their terrorism and turning a blind eye. And when he had escaped the two oversized bullies and made it home in one piece, his dad had slapped him around the head and called him a big girl's blouse for not standing and fighting.

He was the running joke with his dad's mates, they would call him Ryana. Uncle Billy used to take it one step further, force him to parade around naked with his dick tucked between his legs whilst he fumbled at something in his trousers.

They were all there, gathered around him, jeering, laughing, taunting. His dad and Uncle Billy were in cahoots with Tony Lyons and Freddie Lucas and they'd all call him Ryana whilst he danced like Buffalo Bill and they fidgeted around in their pants like they'd lost something.

Ranga wakes up on the stinking floor, sweating profusely, an oppressive weight on his chest. A fat ginger cat hisses at him for having the audacity to gain consciousness. It swats his hand when he pushes it off.

He's burning up; he doesn't know what the fuck G gave him, other than that, it has taken the pain away, if only the physical.

It's getting dark and G is nowhere to be seen, but he knows what's expected of him if he's going to crash here for a few days. Ranga forces himself to a seated position and ignites the torturers in his head.

Get up, you big girl's blouse, his father says, voice laden with gravel. *Stand up and fight.*

Dance for Uncle Billy, Ryana, comes his uncle's slimy, breathless whisper.

"Got to get my shit," Ranga says aloud to drown out his internal riot. He needs to get his things from Philippa, sober up, and find somewhere else to live.

Story of your fucking life.

"Yeah, Dad, I know."

You don't have to take this shit.

It's the voice he's heard before, the one he thought was his father's, but now that he has the whole fucking shebang screaming for joy on the magic roundabout, he can tell it isn't. There are more than a few differences between the two male voices. He wonders who this other phantom is, wonders if it's someone he's forgotten about.

Don't go down without a fight.

This voice is more tangible than the others, as though he's right there behind his shoulder giving him a bit of friendly advice, man-to-man. *Think about what you done this afternoon.*

He pictures the bloke in the toilets.

The old bill will find out it's you that done it. You think that silly tart hasn't told them about you yet?

He's going down, he knows it. Something akin to bliss envelops him at that thought, that finally, *finally,* the inevitable will happen. He's always known he'd end up inside, is surprised it's taken this long.

Fight your own fights, his dad pipes up.

Maybe he really hasn't got a dick between those legs, says Uncle Billy.

"I fucking have!" Ranga says, grabbing at himself through wet trousers.

That's right, boy. You have. Go and show them bitches what's for. Get them out of my house.

Ranga runs from G's place, a human firework, a man on fire.

Watch Out

The smudging stick Niamh hands her gives off a weird funky aroma but it's not half as annoying as her hatred for the smell of marijuana. She shows her what to do, wafting the smoke rising from it, dispersing it with her fingers. The house is blessed by the holy glow of dozens of candles and smouldering incense sticks. Niamh grinds the two Baoding balls around and around the palm of her hand, allowing their rhythmic chimes to become the background to the coming mantra. Niamh nods to Philippa, who wafts the smoke from her burning joint of dried sundries.

"This is not your house."

After a few false starts they begin to speak in unison, starting from the back door and working their way around each space clockwise.

"This is not your house."

They go into the bathroom first and circle the small room three times.

"You know I thought something would happen," Philippa whispers. "Like the house would go all Amityville or some shit."

Niamh smiles but does not break from her chanting.

"This is not your house."

When they enter the kitchen, Layla looks up, hopeful, from a spot in the corner, her nose twitching at the alien odours.

"This is not your house."

As they navigate the kitchen, the strength of citronella attacks them so strongly their eyes water.

"It's working," Niamh says.

"This is not your house."

Philippa feels bad for ridding the place of Vera's spirit but Niamh has said it will probably be an all-or-nothing cure. "It's time to move on, Vera."

"This is not your house," Niamh says, sticking to the one sentence script.

Vera's essence wraps them like a gentle, pre-summer breeze, full of the promise of joys to come. They feel her love physically and emotionally. Tears well in Philippa's eyes. Is this her saying goodbye?

When they step over the threshold to the living room, the onslaught of Roger's presence knocks them back as if it were a solid object.

"Jesus Christ." Philippa coughs, retches, and almost drops the smudging stick. Her lungs fill with tobacco smoke and the rancid tang of old man sweat.

"Fuck," she hears Niamh mutter, and that worsens her fears. They retreat to the kitchen. "Cover your mouth and nose. He's going to use everything he has against us, which means he knows it will work."

Niamh pockets the Baoding balls and they put their hands over their mouths and noses and venture back into the maelstrom, sticks circling the air.

"This is not your house."

"This is not your house."

"This is not your house." They naturally progress to shouting as the stench grows.

Philippa gasps when she feels something whip the burning parcel from her fingers and throw it behind the settee. Layla is going mental in the kitchen but will not cross into the room. Niamh grips onto her smudging stick with both hands, an unseen wind blasting at her black curls. "This is not your fucking house!"

The already broken plasma TV rattles on the wall and they watch as the fixings unfasten and it smashes to the floor. Anything that's loose is hurled at them as if they're being assaulted by an angry child. "He's not strong enough," Niamh laughs. The throws are on target but there's not enough power behind them to hurt.

Still the candles in the room snuff out and Philippa feels invisible hands poking at her breasts and buttocks.

"This is not your house." She screams. She feels him grab her with more zest, more pressure. "Neem, it's not wor—"

She's yanked on to the sofa and her arms are pinned to her sides. Niamh dives in to help but is thrown back into the fireplace.

"Shit!" Niamh's face rocks from side to side. Philippa hears the thwack of slaps and sees her cheeks begin to bloom.

"This is not your...oh fuck it!" Philippa squints her eyes against the stinging tears and begins to bellow. "That's it! Another fucking man, overpowering another fucking woman. Get with the fucking times, you senile old cunt!"

Niamh looks at her in bewilderment before something resembling a grin rises to her swelling lips. "Yeah, it's fucking 2022, bitch, times have moved on and so should you."

"Us women have learned how to fucking hit back. We..." Philippa can't think of anything to say.

"We have programmes that empower women now, we aren't just 'her indoors' or 'a bit of skirt'."

"Yeah!" Philippa laughs and she feels him weaken for a second. They're getting to him. "We've got a female fucking Doctor Who now, for fuck's sake!"

"Men," Niamh butts in, "even bitter old dead ones, can't tell us what to do anymore. I'm a woman. I don't give a fuck what you think makes a woman. I think like a woman, I act like a woman, I fucking feel like a woman. I *am* a woman."

"Vera!" Philippa screams, "stand up to him! We are one, you don't have to take his shit anymore. He is nothing. Just a pathetic man, nothing else."

For a few seconds they feel his power strengthen even more but then the smell of citrus fruits begins to intermingle with the old man stench.

"It's working!" Philippa shouts. "This is not your house anymore, you can't behave like this. We won't let you get away with it. I'll find your fucking grave and plaster ABBA pictures all over it!" Thinking of ABBA brings back memories of childhood birthday parties, which almost always consisted of just the two of them in their bedrooms, eating crap, but they were happy times with the only person she's ever truly been happy with.

Roger's hold over them begins to loosen. Niamh gets up as soon as she can and frantically relights the candles and incense. "You're a piece of shit. I hope to Christ you never had any kids, as they would be ashamed of you." This clearly hurts as Niamh has the firelighter snatched from her fingers.

"Oh my God, I bet he was a Jaffa," Philippa whispers, and laughs at Niamh's look of confusion. "A seedless orange. The old bastard fired blanks, I'd bet money on it."

"Oh, wow. Is that it? Is that why you're such a bitter old cunt? What, couldn't you keep it up or something?" Niamh picks up the lighter. "Ha! I bet I'm more fertile than you and I have a zero sperm count!"

Philippa is free; she picks up her still burning smudging stick and cackles.

"It's fear." Niamh is wild-eyed, possessed by her own rage. "Men have been scared of women since Adam. You're scared of us being out of your control. It just makes your dick wilt even more. You want the power, even when you're fucking dead."

It's true. Philippa knows it is. It is all men. Even her own father liked to be in charge. Always planning everything, telling her and her mum what to do, but at least he was decent enough when they disagreed, wasn't a manipulative, abusive old bastard.

"As for **gender**, man you're so out of touch," Niamh screams, as she thrusts flames against wicks. "Anything goes now, and let me tell you something, at this precise moment, whatever the fuck you are, you have no gender. You were a man but you're not now, not that much different from me."

"There's so many terms you need to catch up with." Philippa knows what they're really doing is bombarding the entity with so much information that they can overpower it. "LGBTQIA-plus!" she suddenly blurts, hoping like hell she'd got all the letters in the right order. "I bet you wouldn't be able to spell *that* out on the Ouija board, you dirty old bastard."

The conflict of presences sends waves of euphoria and black depression through them, and even through the dog, who chases her tail one second and then growls like her ancestors the next. Philippa helps light the candles on the windowsill, while Niamh rants about the Salem Witch Trials. The net curtains are tied up to avoid being a fire hazard, so she sees Ryan's face quite clearly the split-second before he smashes a brick through the glass.

I Can Be That Woman

She thinks it's poltergeist activity, that the supernatural forces have reached a violent crescendo, until she sees the scrawny figure throw itself through the shattered glass. Philippa drops to the floor, a brick to the side of her head, and Niamh's immediate reaction is to rush to her aid.

A white blur rushes past her and launches itself at the intruder. She knows it's Ryan but doesn't see his face clearly until he stands up fully, Layla hanging off his arm, her jaws clamped on an already bandaged wound.

Her defences kick in and she gets ready to fight, but the tobacco-and-old-man reek is stronger than ever and a buzzing fills the room. She shrieks out as invisible needles, coated in venom, prick her arms and legs. They distract her, and in her disorientation, Ryan does something that makes the dog scream and drop to the floor.

She sees the knife in his hand, slick and red, but will not let him hurt Philippa.

She tries once more to ready for his attack.

Her instincts reminded her how to apprehend a knife-wielder, but they never catered for a counter-attack by a swarm of ghost wasps.

They sting at her face and she can feel them in her hair and Ryan's punch comes out of nowhere, fast and hard, brutally hard.

Giddy, she spins and collides with a door post, her only intention to lead him away from Philippa.

She staggers through the kitchen, still swatting at the insects, lips squeezed shut for fear they'll find entrance there, and he's on her.

They smack to the lino and he rolls her over, pinning her hands above her head.

There's something in his eyes, something extra that she's not noticed before.

He's taken something.

She fights back with her legs but once he's in between them, she knows she's lost. He grins like the devil, impervious to the attacking swarm, drops the knife to the floor, and yanks his tracksuit bottoms down.

"I'm going to fucking kill you," he froths, and rips at her shorts. When he gets them half-mast and frees a leg to get them off, she strikes out with her foot, catching him in the shoulder. He yells in rage, punches her in the centre of the forehead, and everything goes dark grey and swimmy.

There's a vague knowledge of him ripping her shorts and knickers down, and then, as she falls down the tunnel of unconsciousness, his look of horrified confusion, disgust.

Like an Angel Passing Through My Room

The air is alive with the hum of something insectile. Invisible barbs prick at Philippa's flesh and bring her round. She is woozy, her forehead throbs, and blood leaks down over her face. Ryan is still ranting and raving in the middle of the living room, oblivious to the buzzing, the stinging, and the swirling conflicts of citrus and tobacco. His arm is bleeding and he's screaming obscenities up at the ceiling.

"Fuck you and your fucking house!" He swats the fireplace, clear of the makings of Niamh's cleansing kit. Burning aromatic oils and lighted candles are strewn everywhere. Her hearing is muffled by the clout from the brick, but Ryan doesn't even sound like himself now. He's flailing his arms around the place in a frenzy. He wears nothing from the waist down and his dick is standing up.

"What the fuck have you done?" she yells, ignoring the constant lances piercing her skin, and crawls across the room towards the bathroom.

"Oh, my poor sweet angel," she moans, as she passes Layla. She is still alive and yowling at a long slash in her belly. Ryan's got a knife and she has to get out, but she's not leaving until she finds Niamh, even if the worst has happened. She grabs onto the worktop and forces herself to stagger across the kitchen, when she sees Niamh's slender hand flopped on the bathroom floor in a pool of blood.

She vomits when she sees the mass of destruction on the tiles. Clumps of purple hair and scalp lay all over the bathroom, Niamh's dress has been torn away completely, and she's been beaten to a bloody pulp. Her genitals have been stomped on and crushed, just like her pretty face. There's so much blood. Too much blood that Philippa doesn't believe her eyes when she moves.

"Fuck you, you old cunt!"

The voice that bellows from the living room is an angry old man's, thick with the catarrh of a rampant smoking habit. "Kindling! That's what this is. I'll show you."

Philippa wraps a towel around Niamh and lifts her to her feet, thankful that her friend has always been on the petite side and that she has always been big and broad. Niamh's barely conscious, so she flings her almost lifeless body over her shoulder in a fireman's lift, makes for the back door, and freezes.

It's night-time but the kitchen is full of sunlight.

There are tiny flowers in the air, like walking through a forest of cherry trees shedding their bloom. Layla is on her feet and facing the living room, blood freely running from her stomach.

The living room is a bombsite. Ryan stands in the centre, naked, his dick standing up, and the sofa is on fire behind him. Smoke curls around him and it's filled with wasps. The knife that he used to slash his own dog juts from his hand.

He looks at her with more hatred than she could have ever earned in their time together and says, "You were never any good."

He steps into the kitchen, and in an explosion of summer love, Layla launches at him, sinks her teeth into his genitalia, and man and dog both fly backwards into the burning settee. The door slams shut of its own accord and the Bluetooth speaker suddenly cries, "Chiquitita, you and I cry. But the sun is still in the sky," before it, too, succumbs to the fire, which consumes everything in the room.

She carry-drags Niamh towards the back door and the tears and words are a continuous babble.

"Please don't die. You're the only thing in my life that's consistent. I need you; I want you; I love you. I've come to realise that it's a different sort of love, it's taken me years to come to terms with it in my head but seeing you like this... I can't live without you. I don't care about sex or physical gender or any of that shit anymore, love is way deeper than that. I don't care what's between your legs, all I know is no matter how long I've known you, the warmth in your eyes and the brightness in your heart, your smile, has never ever changed. Please don't die. I want to be with you, all the time. FLUID, that's a word you use a lot. We can be gender fluid together. Okay, I don't really know what that means.

"Oh God, I just want you in my life every day. I love you and would do anything for you. One of the reasons I've never been happy with any man is because none of those men have been you. And I know you'd slap me if you could for saying that and I promise if you just wake up you can owe me one.

"Oh God, Neem, I don't even know how that will work out for either of us, fuck, you can't even tell me how you feel at the moment, fuck.

"I'd share the same body with you, haunt me. I want your leftovers, oh my fucking God, that sounds so perverse, but I don't give a shit. If you die, possess me, there's more than enough room. Please, Neem, don't leave me, be with me forever. I'm sorry. I'm sorry this happened. Please. "

"Phil?" Niamh muffles into her back. Philippa kicks open the back door and goes into the night.

Her house is on fire.
Her life is on fire.
Her soul is on fire.
Her heart is on fire.
But she has escaped and is outside, beneath the darkening sky, on dog-shit-covered dead grass, and it doesn't matter; she's with her best friend and their possibilities together are as infinite as the stars above.

Matthew Cash

Author Biography

Matthew Cash, or Matty-Bob Cash as he is known to most, was born and raised in Suffolk, which is the setting for his debut novel Pinprick. He is compiler and editor of Death by Chocolate, a chocoholic horror Anthology and the 12Days: STOCKING FILLERS Anthology. In 2016 he launched his own publishing house Burdizzo Books and took shit-hot editor and author Em Dehaney on board to keep him in shape and together they brought into existence SPARKS: an electrical horror anthology, The Reverend Burdizzo's Hymn Book, Under the Weather* Visions from the Void ** and The Burdizzo Mix Tape Vol. 1.

He has numerous solo releases on Kindle and several collections in paperback.

Originally with Burdizzo Books, the intention was to compile charity anthologies a few times a year but his creation has grown into something so much more powerful *insert mad laughter here*. He is currently working on numerous projects; The Day Before You Came is his sixth novel

. *With Back Road Books

** With Jonathan Butcher

He has always written stories since he first learnt to write and most, although not all, tend to slip into the many-layered murky depths of the Horror genre.

His influences ranged from when he first started reading to Present day are, to name but a small select few; Roald Dahl, James Herbert, Clive Barker, Stephen King, Stephen Laws, and more recently he enjoys Adam Nevill, F.R Tallis, Michael Bray, Gary Fry, William Meikle and Iain

Rob Wright (who featured Matty-Bob in his famous A-Z of Horror title M is For Matty-Bob, plus Matthew wrote his own version of events which was included as a bonus).
He is a father-of-two, a husband-of-one, and a zookeeper of numerous fur babies.

You can find him here:
www.facebook.com/pinprickbymatthewcash
https://www.amazon.co.uk/-/e/B010MQTWKK
www.burdizzobooks.com

Other Releases by Matthew Cash

Novels

Virgin and the Hunter
Pinprick
Fur
Your Frightful Spirit Stayed
The Glut
The Day Before You Came

Novellas

Ankle Biters
KrackerJack
Illness
Hell, and Sebastian
Waiting For Godfrey
Deadbeard
The Cat Came Back
KrackerJack 2
Werwolf
Frosty
Keida-in-the-Flames
Tesco agogo

Short Stories

Why Can't I Be You?
Slugs and Snails and Puppydog Tails
Oldtimers
Hunt The C*nt

Clinton Reed's FAT

Anthologies Compiled and Edited by Matthew Cash &
Em Dehaney

Death by Chocolate
12 Days: STOCKING FILLERS
12 Days: 2016 Anthology
12 Days: 2017
The Reverend Burdizzo's Hymn Book
Sparks
Welcome To A Town Called Hell
VISIONS FROM THE VOID (with Jonathan Butcher)
Under the Weather (with Back Road Books)
Burdizzo Mix Tape Vol.1
Beneath The Leaves

Anthologies Featuring Matthew Cash

Rejected For Content 3: Vicious Vengeance
JEApers Creepers
Full Moon Slaughter
Full Moon Slaughter 2
Freaks
No Place Like Home: Twisted Tales from the Yellow Brick
Road
Down The Rabbit Hole: Tales of Insanity

Collections

The Cash Compendium Volume 1
The Cash Compendium Continuity
Stromboli And Other Sporadic Eruptions

Printed in Great Britain
by Amazon